By Maria Simon

I'll Always Walk Your Fish with You

Who She Should Be

Who She Should Be

a novel

Maria Simon

Acknowledgements:
Used with Permission and Fair Use

Deng Ming-Dao, *365 Tao: Daily Meditations*, Harper Collins, 1992

Kahlil Gibran, *The Prophet*, Alfred A. Knopf, Inc, 1993

Ellen LaConte, *On Light Alone*, Loose Leaf Press, 1996

Trina Paulus, *Hope for the Flowers*, Paulist Press, 1972

Original Manuscript printed in Thailand 2014

Copyright © 2014 Maria Simon

ISBN-13: 978-0-692-23040-4   (Maria Simon)
ISBN-10: 0692230408

Graphic Design: Julie Simon

Photography: Jennifer Morrow

for Dad,

Major General James Elias Simon

and for those who loved him

for Paula,
whose loving hands have
gently healed so many

& for Deena,
whose strength, class, and sunshine-filled
spirit make her a Real princess

Mary Magdalene went to the tomb and saw the stone had been rolled away. She stood there crying, and as she wept, she saw two angels in white sitting where Jesus' body had been. When she turned around, Jesus was standing in front of her, but she did not recognize him; she thought he was the gardener. Then Jesus simply said, "Mary," and she turned towards him and cried out, "Teacher!"

– John 20: 1-16

February 29th – a day of grace; a gift

One day in the morning light

The lotus will open wide

And from its petals sigh

Hallelujah

Chapter 1

FIRST VISIT

The needles pierced my skin ever so gently, gliding in on the width of a single hair. There was a momentary pinch, like hot oil being sprinkled on my back, but then immediate release. My body began to buzz, instantly, and energy radiated every cell of my being, all the way down to my fingertips.

I turned my head towards the wall, careful not to move my body too much or to let my hair fall over my back, and I readjusted my cheek against the pillow. As the buzzing evolved into a subtle hum, I closed my eyes. Deeper and deeper I relaxed into myself; the light February showers tapping against the single-paned window no longer noticeable.

"Ok," I heard her say softly – her work for today now done. She quietly left the room, careful not to slam the heavy wooden door that creaked every time it moved. Old houses are like that.

I laid there, motionless, for several minutes; my breathing becoming heavier. The room stayed silent and still, but for some reason I didn't feel alone. I was convinced nothing was happening, and then all of a sudden *the cabin appeared on the horizon.*

Chapter 2

YELLOW PANSIES

I have a mustard seed & I'm not afraid to use it *was painted in yellow on a little wooden sign outside the cabin door. I couldn't help but to smile; I loved them both at first sight – the sign and the cabin. Having grown up in a Protestant family, I knew well the parable of the mustard seed. Simply put, having faith the size of a tiny round speck is enough to move a magnificent mountain. I took it as a sign that this was the right cabin for me.*

15

When I set out on this journey, I had no idea where it was going to take me, nor how long I would be gone. But most of all, I had no idea what I would discover while I was away. All I knew was that I needed time to stand still for a while, and I needed to listen to myself. It had been so long since I was able to hear the voice of my own soul, and I was missing her.

I was exhausted, literally spent, and I didn't have the first clue on how to bring fresh air back into the space around me. Life does that to us, it crowds us with noise and distraction, it wears us down, and before we know it, we are lost even while sitting in our own homes. And so, I just up and left one day. I didn't tell anyone I was going. I didn't even pack a bag.

The cabin I found sat diagonally along Timberlane Beach. It was situated out on a point, with sand running in each direction leading up to the little house. There were no other cabins nearby; in fact, there were no other people around either. A blonde colored dog roamed along the shore and ended up becoming my faithful companion during my stay. I called her "Sandy."

Wild sea grass in shades of grey-blue and cream grew tall near the house and along the water's edge, and shells tanned themselves in the sun wherever they pleased. The wind blew, the waves rolled, and at night the stars were bright and plentiful. It was serenity.

The cabin itself was weather worn, but quite livable. At one time it must have been painted white with dark blue trim, but the paint had been chipping away for years, and the warm sun had softened the blue. Hardwood floors welcomed my bare feet, and the floor to ceiling windows opened to a magnificent view. You could actually feel the salt being carried from the sea on the morning breeze. The house was actually just one large room with an adjoining outdoor bathroom. Surrounded by plants, I would bathe under blue skies in the morning and under the stars at night.

The main room was sparse, but tastefully decorated with items that caught my eye and drew me in their direction. The minute I opened the front door, I couldn't help but to hear the white down comforter directly opposite me calling my name. When was the last time I had gotten a decent amount of sleep? I couldn't recall. I skipped right over to the rot iron bed and threw myself down on the fluffy mattress. I could have stayed there forever. The waves from the sea were lulling, and peace wrapped its arms around me.

Across the room from the bed was the only other piece of comfortable furniture. An overly stuffed arm chair that had clearly been loved over the years faced out towards the waves. The cushions sagged slightly, and the linen fabric was darker in the back than in the front; the sun had once again left its mark. Somehow I just knew this chair and I would become good friends. On the wall behind the chair was a wooden bookcase filled with all sorts of novels and other creative works. Blank notebooks and unused diaries piled on top of one another, and a box of candles sat on the top shelf.

In place of a kitchen, it had a hot water kettle and a small box of teas. The scent was unrecognizable but comforting. A lone cup and saucer with yellow painted pansies sat on the shelf, along with one tiny silver spoon. The pansies made me smile; they were joyful. For some reason this place was all I needed.

Lying on the window ledge near the chair was what looked like a bunch of colorful shells. As I finished my small tour, I walked over to them, realizing that what had actually caught my eye was sea glass – beautiful light blue, pale yellow, ivory, sage, and lavender sea glass. The pieces were small and well smoothed from years of tumbling through rough waves. Each piece had been pierced and strung in a pattern with tiny shells. One piece of sea glass and then ten small shells; each with a knot in between and repeating five times. It was quite pretty, and looked like a necklace. It had one large loop, which I figured was for putting over your head, and then a clear piece of glass, similar in shape to a heart, followed by a tail. However, I could clearly see the loop wasn't large enough to fit over any adult. And then it hit me; it was a rosary – a rosary from the sea.

I laid the ocean gems back along the ledge and spent the rest of the afternoon perusing the bookshelf. Several titles were familiar, but most of them were new to me. Classics, novels, books from different faiths and traditions, gift books, children's books, and some books with nothing but pictures. I was most intrigued by those. I plopped down into the cozy chair and flipped through a few just to have a peak. The visuals looking back at me made my heart feel lighter, and I noticed I was easily losing myself within the pages. It was like there was this whole other world in there waiting for me. After a few minutes, I closed the book and put it back on the shelf. I walked towards the window and looked out as far as I could; the edge of the sea was unreachable. I took in a deep breath and held it, and then I slowly let it escape.

Turning back around, my eyes slowly moved over every detail of my new little space. This was where I was going to be spending my days and my nights. This was where I was going to meet up with myself again. There was no one here but me, I had all the time in the world, and I was safe.

That was it. There was no television or computer; no radio, phone, or even a deck of cards. It was a one room cabin on the beach, filled with books, shells and tea. It was perfect, and it had been waiting for me.

Chapter 3

30 MINUTES EARLIER

My bones literally ached from the damp chilling weather that refused to leave in order to make room for spring. With each passing year, winter crept longer and longer into February, and sometimes even into March, robbing us of the frilly pastel dress-wearing days I remembered as a child, when all the church school kids couldn't wait for Easter to arrive. At that age, chocolate bunnies were a bit more exciting than the resurrected

Jesus, who incomprehensibly had just been born three months earlier.

Bitterly cold wind shook the bare limbs of trees and neighborhood cats roughed it with slight scowls across their faces as I pulled up to the vintage home on "D" Street. It hadn't been difficult to find. I parked my car on the side of the road and came around to the front of the grey, two-story house. Its broken down concrete steps and sagging front porch showed their years, but the garden, though stunned by winter, clearly made up for it.

Lavender bushes, minus their purple flowers, lined the walkway to the front steps, inviting me to lean down and caress their leaves. I brushed my hands against the greenery and then held them to my face, inhaling the sweet perfume my fingers had collected; my hope for spring's return once again revived.

I was just about to walk up the steps to the front door when my eye took notice of a middle aged man tending to some of the hedge around the corner of the house. His head stayed down, covered with a wide brim hat, so I never saw his face. But just as I was about to dismiss him, he tilted his head slightly in my direction and nodded. I returned the gesture with an unenthusiastic grin, and then turned the handle of the front door.

Chapter 4

1 HOUR LATER

Without opening my eyes, I came back to the small room. I heard her open the door once again, with its famous creak and jolt as the handle turned. I kept my eyes closed, but I could tell she was standing over me, delicately feeling each needle for its resistance. My body held them tightly; refusing to let go.

"Not quite yet," she said, "a little while longer." She cranked up the electric heat lamp, which had already turned itself off, and repositioned it directly over my back once more.

I took a deep breath and sighed even lower into my pillow; my face still turned towards the wall. It only took a few moments before *the sand appeared.*

Chapter 5

CRABS

I stepped out onto the beach and noticed Sandy had found a visitor. A middle aged man, probably about sixty, with a strong build and bear like arms was bending over and admiring something along the shore. He looked like the kind of man who was of the "favorite uncle" sort; you just wanted to go up and give him a hug.

His fingers were at work, clearly tying or untying something, and his concentration was steady. Sandy sat beside him, obediently – tail wagging and with a slight pant of breath.

I tossed aside my shoes and headed out. Wrapping a white shall around my shoulders and sheltering my skin from the morning breeze, I continued along the beach to where they were crouching.

This was the first person I'd seen since arriving at the cabin, and by the looks of things, he was no stranger to Sandy. As I approached them, the man looked up; he brushed his hands along his pants and stood upright. He didn't say anything at first, but a sincere smile reflected from his face, especially from the lines around his eyes. Sandy stood up on all four legs, her tail wagging even faster, as if she had been waiting for this introduction.

"Hello," I called out, still clutching my shawl.

"Good morning," the man replied. "It's a beautiful day, isn't it?"

I took in a deep breath and then let it out slowly.

"Yes, yes it is. I imagine every day here is beautiful," I said.

The man smiled, thoughtfully.

"What are you looking at?" I asked, dropping my gaze to the sand and rocks near his feet. I bent down to take a closer look.

"Crabs," the man replied, showing me the web of knots the small creatures had been caught in. "They seem to have gotten themselves stuck."

Trash and other debris had formed a strangling mess, and the handful of crabs trapped in it were helpless. The garbage was pretty disgusting, especially the broken pieces of glass and algae covered boards, and I honestly couldn't figure out why the man was working so hard at it. Who in their right mind would want to touch what had washed up on shore?

"Why don't you just leave it?" I asked; my nose scrunched up from the slightly sour smell. "It's really not *worth it if you cut yourself, and besides, a few crabs aren't going to make a difference."*

As I finished my plea, the man tugged even stronger and tore away some netting that had been trapping the two small creatures. They scurried out towards the nearest rock they could hide under and disappeared.

"Tell that to those two," the man said, and then he walked on to wash his hands in the waves.

I was humbled. I stood there for a moment, rewrapping the part of my shawl that was trying to fly away. I bent down and lifted one of the rocks where the crabs had run to. Under the shelter and shadow of the stones were the two creatures, nestled together and motionless. They were scared – I could see that – and for the first time I realized that even the smallest of us is worthy of grace.

When the man returned, I was already sitting on a log that had weathered years of beatings from the sea. He joined me, rubbing his hands together in an attempt to dry them.

"The name's Jim," he said. "The pup and I (clearly referring to Sandy) are happy to have you join us for a few days. "

"I'm Mary Lou," I replied. "It's nice to meet you, too."

The man smiled and tilted his head in a gentlemanly like fashion.

"Mary Lou," he said.

"I'm sorry about my comments disregarding the crabs earlier," I continued; Jim waited. "I've just never thought much about them before – that's all."

Jim didn't say anything; he just looked at me, giving me his full attention.

"Why did you come here?" he asked.

My eyes dropped to my hands. I honestly didn't know the answer.

"That's ok," he said, taking in a big deep breath of sea air and looking out towards the horizon. He gave me a reassuring smile and gently patted my leg. "I think I have an idea. Meet me back here tomorrow morning and we'll get started."

I was puzzled; "get started" with what?

"Tomorrow morning," he said, as if I hadn't heard him the first time. "Don't forget."

And then he picked himself up from the log we'd been sitting on, grabbed the walking stick that had been lying next to his feet, and headed off in the opposite direction of the cabin, with Sandy joyfully trotting along at his side.

Chapter 6

2 HOURS LATER

"Ping!" the electric heat lamp announced; its timer
having made its way back down to zero. I heard the old
wooden door screech once again, and even before I
opened my eyes, I knew I was no longer on the beach.
What just happened, I wondered? I didn't think I had
actually fallen asleep, and yet, I had clearly been
transported somewhere.

The bitter wind threw rain against the window as I felt the old woman move through the room; the heat lamp being rolled away. Her hands quietly made their way over the landscape of my back, pinching off each needle which was now ready to release. She reached over to the side table and grabbed a white tissue, which she dabbed over a few spots; apparently a bit of bleeding can happen some times.

"Take your time getting up," she softly said. "I'll see you next time," and then she closed the door behind her.

My face was still lying against the pillow, facing the wall to my right. I lifted it gently, in awe of how heavy my body felt, like it was sinking into the table, and I turned to face the other direction. On the opposite wall was a red and gold Asian print. The characters where ones I couldn't read, but I thought the faces of the two dancing Chinese children, along with the interwoven dragon and phoenix, were beautiful. Sacred prayer beads and origami cranes hung from a few jagged nails, and the small table near the window held a bowl of dried herbs that had been partially burned.

I moved my limbs and joints, inhaling deeper as I gathered myself up from the table. My body felt wiped out, but it also felt peaceful. There were no aches or pain, not even any soreness where the needles had gone in. I did, however, feel like I had just been through a huge ordeal, though I couldn't really tell you what had happened.

Eventually I sat up straight on the table, moving my neck to the right and then the left; the stiffness it had carried earlier was no longer there. I slid down to the floor and began collecting my clothes from the corner, placing one cotton layer over my head and then another, and lastly tying a handmade knitted scarf around my neck. It had been a gift from my sister.

I refolded the light-blue fleece blanket that had been covering my legs for the last two hours and placed it at the foot of the bed, and fluffed the pillow I'd been sinking into as an afterthought. Then I wrapped my coat around me before opening the door and heading back out into the cold March wind.

Chapter 7

2 WEEKS BEFORE

The lump showed up on the morning of February 29th – Leap Day. I had already taken my shower and was nonchalantly massaging moisturizer over my skin when I first noticed it. I paused – I wasn't shocked or upset – I think in some ways I even expected this would eventually happen to me.

I quietly held my breath for a moment, staring at my reflection in the bathroom mirror. If I just stood still, maybe I could figure out what I was supposed to do next. Finally I took a deep breath, continuing to keep calm, and I just kept staring.

I touched the lump a few more times, just to make sure I hadn't imagined it, and then I moved my hands away and looked down at my make-up case. There was nothing I could do about it at that moment, and I was late for work already; I would deal with it all later. Or maybe, just maybe, it would go away.

So, I picked up my case of eye-shadow, rubbed the small brush through the powder, and continued to get ready for the day. Why worry about tomorrow when I couldn't even deal with today?

My Monday morning administrative team meeting went long that morning, cutting into my already short lunch break. Deadlines and office politics where nothing less than a migraine headache worth of stress, which had been haunting my temples, neck and shoulders for as long as I could remember. You know something's out of balance when your top drawer at work holds three different types of Costco-size pain killers.

Throughout the morning I found myself checking the size of the lump, just to see if by any chance it had decided to go down. But no such luck. When I got home that day, I poured myself a tall glass of red wine – the cheap stuff that comes out of a box, another treasure from Costco – and I drowned any fears that were sitting on the surface while watching sitcom reruns and finishing off the left over pizza from the night before.

At two-thirty in the morning, I peeled myself off the couch and put myself to bed. There was no point taking a shower or changing my clothes, I was too wiped out. All I wanted was to sleep in my bed; comfortable pillows and a down comforter. I was already sleep deprived from too many evenings at the office and nagging late night phone calls from my boyfriend – who felt the need to call repeatedly and discuss every flaw in our relationship (apparently I wasn't living up to his preconceived fantasy of what the ideal girlfriend should be.) I was obviously a disappointment – so thankfully, the wine had successfully done its duty.

The next morning, when I was once again standing in front of the mirror putting on my face cream, I looked down at where the lump was staring back at me. I placed my fingers ever so lightly on top of it, pushing harder than I had the day before, and I felt a wave of panic run down my spine. There was no denying it; something was there.

This time, instead of staying calm, I felt my heart begin to race. Just when I thought my stress level couldn't go any higher, it did; this clearly wasn't helping my blood pressure. It was too early yet for me to truly be scared. I didn't know anything for sure, and I was still leaning on the side of ignorance. I knew better, of course, but it felt safer.

And so I ignored it.

For one week I forced myself to live in complete denial. I didn't mention the lump to anyone, I didn't go see a doctor, and I did everything I could to get it out of my mind. I even stopped touching it. In the mornings, I began getting ready without looking in the mirror, for my reflection staring back at me was simply too much for me to deal with.

Every night I poured myself a huge glass of wine – or two – I turned off the phone, and for six days I was able to convince myself that I was in control of the situation. If I didn't think about, then it couldn't hurt me.

But then one afternoon, for whatever reason – I still don't know what triggered it – the walls of non-acceptance came crashing down. I panicked while sitting at my desk, and tears of anger and confusion slowly started making their way over my cheeks. After all I'd been through the last few years, why was this happening? Why me? Why now?

I called my doctor's office that afternoon and got an appointment for two hours later at 4:30pm. It was the last appointment of the day.

Chapter 8

4:30 P.M.

Visiting the doctor's office never feels good, but at the end of the work day it's even more eerie. Most of the nurses have already left, screaming children are nowhere to be found, and the light of day is just about gone outside the windows that are cooling down with the setting of the sun. It's a cold feeling being there at that hour.

Thankfully, my doctor was professional enough to treat me like the first patient of the morning – not making any sly remarks about wanting to get home nor about my last minute planning; I guess that comes with the territory. I also wasn't a stranger.

Sadly, the one person who knew me more intimately than any other was my doctor. I had been with the same boyfriend for a number of years, but sex is not the same thing as intimacy. In fact, often times they have nothing to do with the other. My doctor, on the other hand – who I was clearly *not* sleeping with – has been a real friend to me over the years. From my mother's unsuccessful battle with breast cancer to my father's drinking habit, and most recently, my high blood pressure and struggle with anxiety, he had been there every step of the way. I just wish our meetings were for more uplifting reasons.

And so, there I was, once again, plopped up on the exam table and picking at the skin around my nails – something I did when I was nervous. I had just been in this same examination room one month prior, getting a refill for the fabulous little blue pills that I was now a slave to every four hours.

Generalized anxiety disorders happen to be more common than most people know. To be clear, anxiety is not the same as depression – though sometimes a person is dealing with both at the same time. With anxiety, the patient doesn't feel sad and suicidal. Instead, there is constant panic and worry that plays over and over in their head. Rational thought no longer sits on the forefront of their mind, and the ability to plan five minutes down the road becomes completely overwhelming. At least that's the way it was for me.

The answer then: these little blue pills. They didn't fix everything, but they sure took the edge off.

My doctor said the surfacing of GAD was completely understandable considering the combination of my mother's drawn out death, my father's drama, my unfulfilling job, and the frailty of eggshells surrounding my relationship. At the same time, he wasn't willing to simply dish out medication on a regular basis; he gave me nine months to take the first major step of either finding a new job or ending my unhealthy relationship. Trying to do both would have been too much.

"One day at a time," he said. "Let's just deal with today."

That was around Thanksgiving, and now we were in the middle of Lent – fifteen days until Easter. Not much had changed in my everyday circumstances. If fact, I think my headaches were possibly becoming more common, if that was even possible. Thus, the reason for the Costco aspirin.

I had just about picked at all the fingers on my left hand when I heard a familiar little tap on the exam room door. That was the doctor's way of letting me know he was on the other side. With his typical up-beat spirit and slightly crooked smile, he opened the door and acted like we were old friends.

"Mary Lou," he stared in. "Great to see you."

For a moment I thought he was out of the loop about why I was there.   I gave him a little smile and nodded in return.

"So I understand we have a little something to check out," he continued, clearly not wasting time for too many niceties. With the most reassuring pearly smile, he set down my file on the counter and came over next to me. "Let's have a look," he said.

I held my breath as his fingers made their way around my breast. Within a matter of moments, his face went from carefree and friendly to serious.

"Yeah, there's definitely something going on here, isn't there?" he stated, perhaps more for himself than for me. "I'll be right back," he said.

The door had only been closed for about a second, if even that, when he quickly swung it open wide and hung the top part of his body back into the room; his hand still on the handle, and his feet planted outside.

"Oh, and just so you know, this shouldn't be as bad as what your Mom had," he said, and then he flashed his trademark smile once again before leaving.

Oh jeez! I hadn't even gone down that road yet, at least not until he said it. A huge wave of panic and fear washed over me, from my head all the way down to my toes. My heart started to palpitate out of my chest, and I wondered if I was having a heart attack. But I knew better, it was just my anxiety acting up.

And then, like a layer of cold cream over a burn, the most amazing calm slowly washed over me. By bringing up my Mom like that, he actually helped me feel closer to her in that moment; it was like my Mom's spirit was there with me.

A few minutes later the doctor walked back in, holding a small piece of note paper in his hand.

"I made you an appointment with a specialist for tomorrow morning," he said. "Eight a.m. We'll just stay positive until we know anything – sound good?" he asked, his smile now a bit less pearly than before.

I wasn't buying it, and I don't think he was either.

Chapter 9

FIRST REFERRAL

As you can imagine, I didn't sleep much that night, despite the two glasses of wine that were becoming a habit. When the alarm finally went off, I dragged myself out of bed and bee-lined it for the top drawer in the kitchen. Ten milligrams of instant relief awaited my arrival. The day I knew all of this was mental was the day I popped the pill and immediate calm spread through me; there was no way the medication could have made it to my blood stream that fast.

The mornings were always the worst for my anxiety; every day felt overwhelming, even before stepping into the shower. And just like clockwork, my body let me know when four hours had passed; it was ready for more pacifying "candy." Though I knew the physical symptoms were nothing more than a reaction to what was going on in my brain, I simply wasn't strong enough to deal with it all – at least not yet. Figuring out what my triggers were and calmly talking myself through moments of challenge would come much later in my remission process. So on that morning in March, I was thankful for the little blue "tool" that was helping me get through.

"Medication is a tool, not a crutch," my doctor gently explained to me. "It shouldn't be abused or cursed, but rather, used in a way to assist you until you are able to assist yourself."

After taking my pill – even before my required cup of strong black coffee – I hurried through my morning routine, careful not to touch my lump more than necessary. I was beginning to feel hatred for it.

I sat in my car in the parking lot of the hospital until the doctor's office opened, and even then, I waited a few extra minutes before walking in.

The receptionist at the front desk was far from friendly; she should have used some extra time looking at the overly large aquarium that all medical offices seem to have before dealing with patients that morning. She took my name – unenthusiastically – and then made me wait. They always make you wait. Aquariums and waiting – the two givens of any doctor's office.

When I finally met the man who would be leading me through the next phase of this less-than-joyous journey, I was shocked. He was a no-nonsense sort of fellow, lacking in the typical small talk of a general practitioner; I suppose that's the prerogative of a specialist. He did, however, make me smile when our introduction included a headlamp plastered to his forehead. A tool of the trade, I assumed.

He shook my hand and gave me his name, and then said we should "get down to business." After a few minutes of examining my chest, he asked me to sit up and began jotting down a list of words on his notepad.

"Here are all the things this could be," he said, very matter of fact. "Our job is to begin narrowing this list down until we know for sure what we're dealing with."

I nodded my head in understanding, trying not to be distracted by his headlamp.

"I'm going to start you on a round of antibiotics, in case this is nothing more than a bad infection. I rather doubt that's what it is, but let's do this anyway, just to be able to rule it out. Again, we're trying to narrow down the list," he repeated, while running his pencil up and down the dotted items.

Fatty tissue was written first, followed by *infection, fibroadenoma, fibrocystic changes*, and *cyst*; the last word on the list was *cancer*.

Chapter 10

WAITING

I honestly believe there is nothing more painful and terrifying than waiting for the unknown. It's the most hopeless, maddening, scary feeling I can recall.

For five days I dutifully took the antibiotics the specialist had given me, while trying to get back to some form of normalcy at work and in my personal life. I didn't tell anyone what was going on; why worry others when it might just be nothing? I didn't say anything to my boyfriend because honestly, I literally couldn't handle the potential of him walking out. And I never breathed a word of this to my Dad, because really, where does one begin?

So I toughed it out alone – for five days – just me and my red wine box from Costco.

I tried to stay positive, though I was scared beyond words, and for a few days I actually thought the size of the lump was going down. When I went back to the specialist after a week's worth of meds, I told him as much. He didn't even humor me.

"Yeah, no," he bluntly said. "I think maybe it just moved around a bit."

I solemnly watched as he marked *infection* off the list.

Chapter 11

THE FIRST NEEDLE

The same unfriendly nurse from the reception area
came into the doctor's office, at the specialist's request, to
escort me to a room down the hall. Before we left, the
specialist handed her a pink form that he'd marked up with
his terrible penmanship, and she ran her eyes over it
before leading me onward. She looked up at him, in
surprise, and he nodded in reply.

Well this can't be good, I thought to myself; my anxiety starting to spin itself into high gear.

Then, as if someone had flicked a magic wand, the nurse turned from cold and uninterested to rainbows and sunshine.

"Mary Lou," she said with her most pleasant voice and smile, "would you please follow me this way?"

Why was she being nice to me all of a sudden?

A reclining chair was waiting for me in some sort of lab facility; at least I was going to be comfortable. The doctor showed up a few minutes later, complete with headlamp and powder-blue plastic gloves, and explained to me about the small procedure he was about to conduct. He said he wanted to biopsy the lump to get a sample of its cells. From there, he said, we would have a clearer picture of where to go next.

"Will it hurt?" I asked him.

"Only a little," he said, "and there might be some swelling afterwards, but it won't be anything a little ice and some pain meds can't fix."

The newly transformed sunshine-nurse explained to me the details of the procedure and numbed the area around the lump. The doctor took a black pen and marked the exact location of where he wanted to biopsy, and then we waited.

Once again, the waiting was killing me. What was the hold up?

"I'm just going to hold off a minute until my lab tech gets back," the doctor said. And then, as if right on cue, the man walked through the door.

The doctor adjusted his headlamp, shining the bright light of authority onto my breast. He told me to take a deep breath, and then he began.

The biopsy needled brushed in and out of the lump, like someone churning butter with a small implement. It didn't hurt so much as it was uncomfortable and invasive. I hated every moment of it; I don't even think I took a breath.

When it was all over, the doctor handed the biopsy needle to the lab tech, and the sunshine-nurse bandaged my wound. She also handed me a bag of ice.

"It will probably bruise," she told me, "and there's a good chance it will swell. It's not going to be happy that someone was in there messing with it."

Ya think?

The doctor and the lab tech stood close together over a microscope, talking in mumbled voices and whispers.

Once again, while holding ice over my anxious heart, I waited.

Chapter 12

RESULTS

A circle was drawn around the last word on the list.

Chapter 13

SILENCE

I don't know how others have dealt with this kind of news. All I know is what I felt when the doctor said it to me: *probably cancer*. It was like a bubble of white cloud came in all around me, blocking out every noise and feeling. My pulse slowed down, along with my breathing, and I felt the tension in my shoulders relax. I wasn't scared. I wasn't even anxious. I was just silent.

Chapter 14

ANOTHER REFERAL

The specialist took off his headlamp for the first time. He sat down next to me with a completely new demeanor and folded his hands in his lap; his toes almost touching mine.

"We still have a lot we don't know yet, so let's not get too far ahead of ourselves," he very calmly said to me. "There are more tests I want to run on the cells, and several options we can talk about after that. But before we start making plans, I have one other thing I'd like to try first," he gently explained.

I still didn't know how to feel at this point, but the reality of my situation sank in a bit. Thoughts of *chemo*, *hair loss*, and *scars* across my chest began playing over and over again in my head. At the time, *death* hadn't even occurred to me – which I'm surprisingly thankful for.

"I know this is all a lot to take in," he continued, "and I want to assure you that we'll be with you every step of the way."

With that he smiled and gave my knee a little pat.

"However, before we discuss any types of possible treatments," he said with a bit of whimsy, "I am going to refer you to one other person."

Oh great, I dreaded, more tests.

He handed me a plain business card. On it was a name I couldn't pronounce and an address on "D" street.

"She knows to expect you," the doctor informed me. "When your time with her is through, come back and see me, and we'll run some more tests. Until then, try not to go too far down the road with all of this. "

I quietly nodded my head in understanding and looked down at the name on the card.

"See you in a couple weeks," he said, as he gathered his headlamp and moved towards the door.

I looked up, sort of in a daze.

"Right," I said to him, a half smile of fake optimism resting on my lips.

Chapter 15

MORE NEEDLES

The thought of willingly inserting needles all over my body had never been something that appealed to me. Acupuncture, and pretty much all forms of alternative medicine, were completely new, and somewhat strange things in my opinion. If this was going to be anything like the biopsy, I wasn't the least bit interested.

But after arriving at the old house on "D" street and noticing the middle aged gardener who attempted to prune in the cold March weather, I made my way to the top of the well-worn steps and opened the squeaky screen door. The house was quiet, except for the trickling sound of water from the rock garden fountain near the foyer. Most of the lights were low, and the walls in the hallway were tall and dark. I took a seat on the wooden bench next to the fountain and waited.

The creak of a door made its way down the hall to where I was sitting, and a very petite Asian woman followed afterwards. She looked as if she were eighty years old; small frame, wrinkled skin, and hair in a tight bun. She didn't say a word, but motioned for me to come with her. I picked up my bag and headed down the dimly lit hall.

A glorified closet is the way I would describe the small room the Asian woman led me to. There was hardly enough room for both of us to be in there. She gestured to the very narrow massage table, which was where I assumed she wanted me to sit, and then sat herself down on a stool in the corner. Neither of us had spoken a word.

Tilting her head to the left and then the right, the small woman stared at me. I was becoming a bit uneasy, so I smiled. She did not.

We sat that way for a few minutes, and then she pointed to my shirt and then the chair; she wanted me to undress. There was a fleece blanket at the end of the table, which she put on my lap, and then she left.

I sat there for a minute and took in a deep breath. What on earth had I gotten myself into? But surprisingly, even though all of this was foreign to me, I felt safe. It was the first time I'd felt like that in a long time. It was like I was tucked away somewhere, some place where no one could find me, and I was protected.

Folding my shirt on the chair, I held the blanket around my chest and jumped back up on the table. The little lady must have heard my movement because she re-entered the room as soon as I sat down. She motioned for me to lay my head on the pillow, face down, and then she readjusted the fleece covering so that it was over the bottom half of my body. Very gently, she swept my hair off to the side, exposing my entire neck and back.

My eyes were facing the wall opposite of where she stood, so I couldn't see what she was doing. However, I heard her crank the timer on what I later learned was a heat lamp, and then rub her palms together underneath it.

All of a sudden, smooth warmth spread all over my skin. The aromatic oils she'd put on her hands made their way all across my back and neck, and their earthy scent wafted through the air. In a sculpting fashion, like a potter working a piece of clay, she massaged the heated oil into my muscles and joints; my eyes got heavy and my mind began to drift.

When my body had completely relaxed, she danced the tips of her fingers over my spine. Like a paintbrush, she dragged them along the muscle and then stopped, ever so gently rocking them back and forth on the locations she paused at. And then like a wave going back out to sea, she slid her fingers out away from my spine and rested on different island points scattered throughout my shoulders and back. As she reached each point, she rocked again, both on her fingertips and her feet.

The crinkling sound of plastic brought me back to the present moment, and then for the first time she spoke.

"Take a deep breath," her soothing voice said to me. So I did. "And again," she added, lining the rhythm of her breathing up with mine.

Together we took a few more breaths, and then I felt the first pinch of a needle on my back as I exhaled.

"And again," she repeated, inserting a new needle on a different part of my back every time I let out my breath.

Surprisingly, I hardly felt a thing until she inserted the last needle right below my shoulder blade. I thought I was going to jump off the table.

"Ahh!" I cried out

"Jtut jtut jtut," she clicked with her tongue, like one does with a crying child, wiggling the skin around the needle to lessen the sting.

"That is your *lung point*," she explained. "Your body is grieving; that is why it suffers."

Quietly she placed the plastic wrapper of unused needles on the side table and struck a match. Slowly and methodically she lit the bowl of herbs, and then blew out the flames so the healing smoke would envelope me. Lastly she rolled the heat lamp over to the edge of the table and positioned it so warmth blanketed over the needles.

"Ok," she said, as a sort of benediction, and then she left, allowing the needles to do their thing.

It wasn't long after that when I first began to *smell the sea breeze*.

Chapter 16

THE SECOND TIME

When I returned to the house on "D" Street the next day, I was a tad bit more relaxed and ready for what was about to take place. My earlier preconceived notions of the pain that piercing my body with all those tiny needles would bring turned out to be false. Instead, I experienced some type of internal and overall peace that I had not intended on feeling.

The old woman was no more friendly the next day, however she refrained from the starring game we had engaged in the day before. Once she led me down the hall to the small room, she asked me how I had slept.

"Quite well, actually," I reported to her, "which completely surprised me since I haven't had a decent night's sleep in ages."

She listened intently, and knowingly nodded her head.

As she rubbed her hands under the heat lamp, I asked her what type of oil she was using; the scent was still unknown to me, yet familiar.

"Sandalwood, bergamot, and geranium," she replied, and then the wave of warm silky fragrance once again washed over my back.

Together we breathed as she prepared each needle; inserting only when my body released with an exhale.

Most of the time I still didn't feel anything; the lung point being the one exception.

"Grief takes time," she simply said, as she witnessed my body clenched under the stab of its pinch.

She positioned the heat lamp, covered my legs, and left the room without making a sound. Since I had some idea of what to expect the second time around, my body fell into a deep state of rest almost instantly. Before I knew it, *the sun was coming up.*

Chapter 17

ROCKS

I watched the sun rise from the cabin's porch. I sat on the floorboards, dangling my feet over the edge, and marveled at the cranes diving for fish in the morning fog. As the wind picked up and the waves pounded harder, a familiar face showed up along the water's edge; there was Sandy, and not far behind her was Jim.

I jumped down from the deck and walked out to where they were, feeling the cool, wet sand squish between my toes. When I got within speaking distance, I noticed Jim was tossing a rock up in the air and catching it.

"Good morning," I called out.

"And a good morning to you," said Jim. "I'm glad to see you came. Here," he handed me the rock, "this is for you."

The stone was small and oval, smooth to the touch and speckled black and white. It was warm, radiating heat, and it felt alive.

"God created many beautiful things," Jim said as he watched me admire the peppery rock, "and it's our job to enjoy them."

My ears perked up, and I thought for a moment before responding.

"I'm not so sure about the God part, but I agree that there are many beautiful things in this world," I said.

Jim silently nodded his head, knowingly, and we continued walking along the beach.

"You see that pup over there?" Jim asked, motioning towards Sandy, "She's part of God. When you step out into the water, and you feel the waves against your skin – that's part of God. When you first got to the cabin and could smell the ocean breeze – that was part of God. In the morning, when you awake and hear the birds crying to one another – that's part of God. And when you can taste the sea salt on your lips at the end of the day – that's part of God."

I stopped walking and just looked at him.

"You feel that heat in your hand right now? – the energy in that rock? – that's part of God, too."

I looked down at the stone again, surprised; I hadn't said anything about the warmth coming from it, and yet somehow he knew.

"God is part of everything," Jim continued, with an all-knowing smile. "You can call God by whatever name you like, but it doesn't change the fact that God is part of everyone and everything; all the beauty that surrounds us, the people in our lives, the gifts in our pathways, and the opportunities that present themselves."

"Why are you telling me all of this?" I asked.

"Because you're looking for answers," he said, "and this is the first answer to the question you are struggling with."

"And what question would that be?" I asked, somewhat defensively.

Jim stopped walking and turned towards me. He gently put his hands on my shoulders and looked me sweetly in the face.

"You want to know the **Secret to Life***," he said. "You want to know how to live a life that's rewarding, full*

*of purpose and leaves you feeling full of joy. That's why
you're here, isn't it?"*

*And just like that, the fog lifted and my journey
began to unfold.*

*Jim nailed it on the head. Before that moment I
couldn't have told you what was wrong with me, and yet
using only a few brief words this man spelled it out.*

*He released my shoulders and stepped back,
waiting for my reaction, while Sandy brushed up against
my leg. I realized I had been biting down on my lip, and
the rock Jim had given me was suffocating in my tightly
formed fist. I took a deep breath and loosened my grip,
looking down at the black and white stone once again.*

*"Who are you?" I asked, as I looked back up at
Jim's face.*

"I'm just Jim," he said, smiling.

*I smiled at his reply and nodded my head in
understanding.*

"Well ok, 'just Jim,'" I replied, which caused him to grin and his eyes to twinkle, "what can you tell me about the secret to life?"

"**Praise God**," Jim said. "That's the very first thing you have to do. When you wake up in the morning, look to the sky and smile; be thankful for another day of living. Feel blessed to live in a place where you're safe and warm and your needs are taken care of. Be grateful for the friends and family who walk your journey with you, and for those who pick you up when you fall. Let your heart be filled with thanksgiving for all the blessings and joys that shower over you each day, and for the gifts of grace and forgiveness when you stumble. Teach your heart to be in a constant state of gratitude, and recognize that no gift is too small to be thankful for. Walk through each day looking for moments of light to celebrate and treasures that are waiting to be found. And when the sun sets, Praise God, again, and rest in a blanket of peacefulness in anticipation of another day of blessings.

"This is where you begin," he said, "so praise God. *Gratitude can take you a long way, and it can produce some pretty magical results. "*

The day quickly turned to night. I sat out on the deck looking at the stars, thinking about Jim's words. I thought about how strange, and yet wonderful, it was to meet him. I thought about the companionship Sandy had given me when I first arrived at the cabin, and of course I thought about the beautiful view.

But then I reached deeper inside of myself and found other moments worthy of praise. I recalled the feeling of peace my body felt when I first saw the vast ocean lying before me. I closed my eyes and remembered the feeling of the breeze blowing my hair and heightening my senses. I imagined the colors of the sea grass and the crisp white sheets of the bed. I even thought about the lesson I had learned that afternoon from the crabs – the one that reminded me that all of life's creatures are precious.

And I thought about what Jim said regarding God;
I could call God by whatever name I wanted. I liked that.

I went inside, ready to surrender to the hours of
sleep, and looked again at the black and white stone
sitting near the bedside. I held it in my hand, feeling its
warmth once more, and then placed it back on the table.

"Praise," I said out loud; the first stone on the path
to Living.

Chapter 18

FIRST STEP

When I walked down the drooping porch steps of the grey house on "D" Street and headed towards my car, I was silent. I don't mean that I wasn't speaking, but rather, my body and mind were simply quiet. I hardly heard the traffic going past, and I didn't feel like I was in any kind of rush to get back to the office. My pace was slightly slower than usual and more methodical. When I reached into my bag for my car keys, I didn't toss items around looking for them, but rather, I gently took my wallet and hairbrush out one by one, and rested them on the roof of my Honda until I found what I was looking for. When I was through, I just as thoughtfully put them back.

Though the absence of noise had somehow surrounded me, my other senses were heightened; the crisp air ever so faintly carried a scent of spring on its wing; the sun, peaking through the clouds, felt decedent on my face as I closed my eyes and gave it my full attention; and the tape that usually played constantly in my mind was simply on pause.

I sat down in the driver's seat and closed the door. Without realizing it, I just stared straight ahead at nothing in particular. A robin in the tree nearby serenaded me with its song, and I slowly tilted my head up and to the left to notice. The little bird continued repeating the same few notes over and over again, lulling me into a type of trance. It was beautiful. With my hands lying loosely in my lap, still holding my keys, I realized I was *experiencing* the little tune, not just hearing it. I felt alive.

Time moved without me realizing it, so I couldn't tell you how long I actually sat there, but when I finally became aware of the fact that the little bird had stopped singing, I also realized the sun had begun to prepare to leave. And so I did the same.

I turned right at the first stop sign and made my way into downtown. I didn't have a clue where I was going; I simply drove. Lights came on all around me, and despite the cold weather, a handful of spring baskets had been put out along the walkway. How they were surviving was beyond me.

I pulled my car into an open space and tied my scarf around my neck before getting out. With my hands tucked into my coat pockets, and my mind free of any agenda, I simply strolled along the sidewalk and admired the window displays to my right. The independent bookstore was clearly highlighting local authors, and the stationary store displayed their Mother's Day frames a bit early.

Since the sun had gone down, the little hairs on my arms bristled, and the shocking cold wind convinced me to step inside the store for a moment. I perused the aisles of paper and greeting cards and consciously took notice of all the vibrant colors and designs shining back at me. I picked up a few cards and admired them for a moment before moving on, and I even held onto one that I just couldn't put down. Why pay for expensive art when you can frame a small print?

As I made my way to the counter, a fabric covered journal caught my eye. It was cream, with little blue and green seashells scattered over top. I wasn't sure what I was going to do with the notebook, but I did feel like I was supposed to buy it.

When I got home about thirty minutes later, I tossed my black high-heels aside and draped my wool coat over the dining room chair. I was about to pour myself a glass of wine – more out of habit than of need – when I realized I actually didn't want one. That was surprising.

Instead, I dropped down onto the sofa and took my two new purchases out of my bag. The card was beautiful – a watercolor painting of a graceful woman sitting on the ground surrounded by butterflies. There were so many colors and shapes of butterflies flying all around her, and she herself even had two wings of her own. She didn't seem to be an angel, however, but rather, some type of maternal figure. The image made me miss my Mom.

I sunk down a little further into the sofa and replayed the afternoon over in my mind. I picked up a pencil and opened the new journal I'd just bought, and turned to the first page. Brushing lead upon the paper, I made a list.

I drew a small dash and then wrote *beautiful greeting cards that catch you by surprise*, followed by *little birds that sing sweetly in the trees*.

I paused for a moment, thinking back to the words that mysterious man, Jim, said to me on the beach. *Gratitude. Praise. God.*

I set the pencil back down on the page and continued writing.

- Having a job – even if it's not my ideal one – when so many others are unemployed

- My doctor – who has been with me for years, and who I trust

- Having access to medical experts– ones who are willing to try alternative ways

- Little blue pills

- Costco wine

- Sitcoms – good for helping turn my mind off and making me laugh

I stopped writing and looked at my list. It's true, they were all things I was grateful for, but they were a bit depressing. So while biting down on the end of my pencil, I thought about it a bit more. I looked around my apartment for inspiration, and then continued.

- Being able to afford heat in the cold weather

- Having a car to take me around town

- Bright colors in shop windows

- The scent of lavender on my hands from the house on "D" Street

- The feel of the warm sun on my face

That last one in particular made me pause and then close my eyes. I transported myself back to the moment in the afternoon when I actually felt the sun shining down on me, and I smiled.

I put my pencil down, keeping my eyes closed, and I brought my hand up to the lump. Resting my palm close to my heart and reliving the feel of the sun on my face, I felt peace.

When I opened my eyes a few minutes later, I looked back over the list I had written. Despite my current circumstances and all their uncertainties, I could plainly see I had things to be thankful for. And that night it didn't even dawn on me that I forgot to take my little blue pill.

Chapter 19

SAND CASTLES

By some miracle, the weather took a huge turn the next day, and the temperature turned itself up a few notches as I drove to my third acupuncture appointment. Little birds chirped outside the window as I laid on the table, and the heat lamp didn't seem like it needed to work as hard as the day before. Within moments of the needles finding their perfect fit, *the reflection of the sun danced on the whitecaps of the waves, as Jim stood next to a rowboat that had washed up on shore.*

"What happened here?" I asked, pointing to the helpless little vessel.

"It's just taking a time-out," Jim replied, with a playful smile across his lips.

"But what will happen to it?" I continued, gesturing around me to the fact that the tide was quite a ways out from shore, and the boat was not something either of us could move.

"You gotta have a little faith," he said, very fatherly-like. "Don't worry, it will be OK."

I stood looking at the boat and then back at the waves hundreds of feet away; I still wasn't buying Jim's assurance.

"You know," Jim started in, "sometimes you have to trust in things you can't see – in things that have no guarantee. That's what it means to **Have Faith**.

"Take this boat, for instance. From an outsider's view, it looks like it's in bad shape – it's stuck, it's alone, *and even if we wanted to, you and I still wouldn't be able to move it. But do you think that little boat is worried about all that? No. You want to know why? Because it has complete faith that later this evening when the sun begins to set, the waters will make their way back towards the shore and lift it out of the predicament it's in. Then it will be back on its little way to wherever it was originally headed. In the meantime, it's taking a break."*

Jim picked up his walking stick and motioned for us to take a stroll, and so, I followed his lead.

"Having Faith is one of the most important secrets to life," he said. "You must understand that everything comes in its own time; we can't rush it. When you plant a seed, you do your best to water it with care and give it the nutrients and sunlight that it needs, and then you step back, you trust, *and you allow it to grow in its own way. The same is true for us… and for our dreams."*

We walked a little further, quietly, and then Jim paused and looked out towards the sea.

"Mary Lou," he said, "I know you're feeling trapped and a bit helpless right now. I know that in some ways you feel like there is no way out. But I'm here to tell you that you are safe, and that you always have been. You just have to believe.

"It honestly doesn't make much difference to me what you have faith in, just have faith in something – God, a higher power, in others, in yourself, or even just the process. Right now you have to decide what you want to do. Do you want to stay or do you want to go? It's that simple."

What was Jim saying to me? Was I actually a writer of my own path? Jim turned and looked at me, leaning both of his hands and his full weight on the walking stick.

"When people hear the word cancer, they so often jump to the conclusion that it must be written with a capital C. But what I'm trying to explain to you is that what we need to do is to bring the Big C down to a 'little

c.' For your Mom, cancer was a battle – something to fight and curse. But for you, I am going to recommend a different route – compassion.

"How you approach the next chapter of your life is all up to you. It's not anyone else's choice but your own. Some will curse God or the world around them; others will be gentle with themselves and the people in their lives. It's your decision."

Jim lifted himself off of his stick and walked some more.

"Don't run away when the going gets tough, Mary Lou," he pleaded. "Instead, plant yourself like a strong cedar. Grow roots deep into the ground when the wind begins to blow, and stand tall; the storm will strengthen you and show you what you're made of. Thank the wind for the lessons it teaches you, and remember that it's only temporary; every breeze always eventually dies down."

At this, Jim stopped and looked me square in the eye.

"You are more powerful than you realize," he said, very seriously. "I'll even go as far as saying you can heal yourself."

My eyes widened, in surprise.

"But you must first block out all the noise going on around you. Forget about it – just drop it completely – and listen. Listen to the still small voice deep inside. Listen very carefully; it's your soul."

"And then what do I do?" I asked, speaking for the first time in the whole conversation.

"You follow it wherever it leads," he answered with a parental smile. "Believe in your visions and your dreams, Mary Lou. Believe in your ideals and in the fantasies that make you giddy." He put both hands on my shoulders, trying his best to make his point. "That's what true Living is all about."

"But what if the ideal is too far away?" I asked. "What if I've spent all this time going in one direction, and the ideal happens to be on the completely other side of the beach? Does that mean I just wasted my life?" The fear of how he might answer kicked my anxiety into gear and my breathing quickened.

"Breathe, Mary Lou." Jim said as he smiled, and all of a sudden, out of thin air, a sandcastle appeared.

"Someone spent a lot of time building this sandcastle," he said, "and my guess is that the tide is not going to spare it when it comes back in to collect the little rowboat. Life is like that. Sometimes we put our whole selves into something for years, and then one day it just isn't meant to be any more. But that doesn't mean we didn't learn something important. Next time, the builder of that sandcastle just might think about adding a moat around her creation."

What Jim was saying made sense, but it was also a lot to take in. My face must have shown it.

"Having Faith means that when you come to the edge of the cliff," Jim continued, while pointing off to the left, *"like that one right over there – and you need to take the next step…"*

"I know, I know," I cut him off. *"I've heard this before. It means there will be something solid to stand on, even if I can't see it with my own eyes."*

Jim stood back a moment, and took a deep breath.

"That's right," he said, his face a bit more subdue.

"But what if there isn't anything there when I take that big step of faith you're trying to get me to believe in?" I asked, skeptically.

Jim waited for me to calm down, and then he simply replied.

"Then it means you will have learned how to fly."

Chapter 20

DECISON

I had a choice to make – did I want to stay or did I want to go? After my Mom died, I no longer feared death. I knew that if something happened to me, she'd be there to welcome me with open arms. At least that's what I believed. So the dilemma wasn't about fearing the afterlife – it was about determining whether I had it in me to stick this out. Did I want to suffer through a job and relationship that were unfulfilling? Did I want to deal with whatever came of my lump? Did I want to go on missing my Mom and feeling like I had no one to confide in? Leaving seemed so much simpler.

All afternoon I thought about this question. I went home early from work and quietly sat in my apartment. I stared at the faces smiling back at me from framed photos, hugged my overly stuffed Winnie the Pooh – another gift from my sister – and when evening came, I put the bear down and walked into the hallway.

Standing in front of the full length mirror, I looked at my chest. I put my hand over my breast and pressed down on it as much as I could, trying to imagine what I would look like without it. I barely fit into a B cup to begin with, so its absence wouldn't be such a big deal. But at the same time, it was part of me – part of my woman-ness.

Would there be a big scar? Would I become unattractive? What if I want to have kids one day – could I? And most importantly, would I be less of a woman?

Energy surged through me as my anxiety ticked away. I tore off my sweater and threw it on the floor; my tank-top and bra followed. Again, I flattened my breast and stared. My breathing quickened and my chest felt like it would explode; my heart just kept on pounding.

I stayed that way for a few minutes, and then I walked into my bedroom. On top of the dresser sat a photo of my mother. In it, she was always smiling. I looked into her eyes and then back down at my chest again, and then I began to cry. As the gentle tears of surrender made their way down my checks, my heart calmed. I sat down on the bed and crossed my arms over my stomach, hugging myself as I sobbed.

I didn't know much, but the one thing I knew for certain was that my Mom had gone too early – too painfully – and I didn't want that for my own life. I wasn't even thirty-five yet; there was still so much for me to do, to experience, to create. None of this seemed fair, but maybe Jim was right – maybe I could have a hand in my own future. I had no idea what it would entail, or how it would play out. But at least I would still be part of this game called life. And perhaps there was a little boat waiting for me, too – just waiting to take me back out to sea. And so, while sobbing half naked on my bed, I made my decision.

Chapter 21

STARFISH

"So you decided to stay?" Jim asked, more as a statement than a question; his face beaming as he reached his hand into the shrubbery near the edge of the cabin.

In some ways it felt like Jim knew what I was going to tell him even before I said the words. Maybe he did know how this was going to play out all along, but he wanted me to figure it out for myself. And just as those thoughts ran through my mind, Jim tilted his head back my direction and smiled.

He pinched off a little violet flower from the bush and handed it to me. Its face was sweet and innocent, and reminded me of when I was a child. My Mom planted these little pansies every year when our local farmer's market would introduce their spring annuals. Sadly, they only lasted a few months, and then they withered away.

But these pansies came from quite a large plant that clearly had been growing for some time.

"I thought pansies were annuals," I said. "I thought you had to replant them each year."

"That might be what's written on the package of seeds," Jim replied. "But no one told that to these flowers. As far as they're concerned, they'd prefer to just keep on growing."

That didn't make any sense to me. Everyone knows that weather changes force some plants to die, including delicate little flowers.

"The cabin must not get much harsh weather," I stated, hoping for a confirmation.

"Oh no," Jim corrected me, "it most certainly does. It gets its fair share of storms and seasons – just like anywhere."

"But then how do these flowers survive?" I asked.

"They carry on because no one told the annuals they couldn't return," he explained. "And that is exactly what you are going to do as well."

My eyes went from skeptical to wide-eyed.

"I am?" I asked, somewhat shocked.

"Yes, you are," Jim said. "Now that you've made the decision to stay, you are going to learn to see life through a new set of lenses. Even if the world is throwing

a hurricane at your doorstep, you are going to **Stay Positive, Always…always**."

"Seriously?" I asked, convinced that Jim was being totally unrealistic.

"Seriously," he replied. "You tell me – what good ever came from negativism?"

He had a point there. But still, being positive all the time? That seemed like a huge order to fill. And yet, the more I thought about it, the more I had to agree with Jim. It's true – I couldn't think of anything good that ever came from being negative. In fact, it usually just made me feel worse.

Jim picked a few more flowers and tied them together with a piece of string. Then he handed me the delicate bouquet and walked towards the shore.

"I know you're worried about becoming disfigured," he said, his eye spotting something along a large rock.

I didn't say anything; I hadn't told anyone about my fear of surgery or disfiguration.

Jim crouched down near the boulder and pointed to a golden starfish that was hanging on for dear life. One of its five arms was much shorter than the other four, and Jim pointed his finger at it for me to notice.

"Did you know that starfish can grow back their arms?" he asked. "It takes time, but they can do it. For them, it's the most natural thing in the world. No one told them they couldn't, and they felt no need to doubt. You should consider approaching life the same way."

He delicately lifted the starfish off the rock and headed towards the waves, releasing it back into the sea.

"It also never hurts to lend a helping hand," he said as he returned to where I stood. "But we'll get to that later. For today, I want you to be like those pansies and starfish – do that which others say you can't, believe that nothing is impossible, and most importantly, Stay Positive, *especially through the storm. Don't worry about what*

science, rules, or history dictate – listen to the cheering coming from your heart; it will guide you all the way.

"Think about all the children and animals that climb to great heights because the thought of falling didn't occur to them. Or the weeds that grow, even though no one watered them. And the bumblebee – flying around with its big 'ole belly – when aerodynamically it shouldn't be able to get off the ground. That's what I want you to do."

"Are you calling me fat?" I asked, a smile forming on my face. Jim chuckled. "I'm just kidding," I followed up, "and I hear you. Bring the Big C down to a little c, right?"

"Ping!" the heat lamp responded, confirming my new-found wisdom.

Chapter 22

PROGRESS

On my way home from the acupuncture treatment, I stopped off at the grocery store. Plastic eggs, plastic grass, and cheap chocolate that tastes like plastic were all on display as I came through the door. Easter decorations were in full swing – including yellow and white forced daffodils wrapped in pastel tissue – and I couldn't help but to think back to the days when my Mom counted out jelly beans for our baskets. My sister and I never fought over such things, but Mom made sure that each of us had the exact same number of colorful candies sitting under whatever stuffed animal happened to be on sale that year.

A lump formed in my throat as I revisited the old memories; thoughts of Mom usually did that, especially around holiday time. It didn't matter if it was Christmas or St. Patty's Day, Mom always made them special; from her paper-maché table displays to her decorative napkins. I swear she had napkins for every occasion imaginable, including Super Bowl Sunday – which was quite a hoot since no one in our family really cared for football. And the best one, still, was when she put beautiful paper napkins out for Thanksgiving, made each of us take notice of them before passing the cranberries, and then collected them back so they wouldn't get dirty. We never let her live that one down.

As I spotted some pink marshmallow Peeps, and remembered they were much cuter than they actually tasted, a thought suddenly occurred to me. I rolled myself over to the front display and filled my cart with two – not just one – bags of seasonal jellybeans, and I threw in a package of bunny napkins for good measure. Then I lightheartedly continued the rest of my shopping. Instead of being sad about the way life had taken a turn, I would celebrate special memories from the past.   And not only that, but I was determined to enjoy all that nasty sugar without worrying for a second about what it would do to my waistline. I was doing what Jim had just taught me, and I must admit, my heart felt lighter. For a few moments, I completely forgot about my lump. By the time I reached the check-out counter and looked at the time, another surprise made me smile; once again, I had forgotten to take my pill.

If that's not living positively, I don't know what is.

Chapter 23

CHANGE

The gardener was trimming back the lavender bushes the next day when I parked my car next to the house on "D" Street. He never looked up from what he was doing, but he gave me a little nod when I said hello as I continued my way up the stairs, and the cat that had once grimaced at me was now curled up on the porch, purring.

Spring does that to all of us – it brings out the sunshine that's been bottled up for so many months. I always laugh when I sit downtown at Brenner's Bagels and watch the changes that go by the window when the temperature warms up a few degrees. Bystanders who were cranky the day before now open the door for strangers, and everyone wears short-sleeves – a few even brave it with flip-flops – though it's a mere 60 degrees outside.

I guess that's why I wasn't completely surprised when the old woman mentioned she could already see a change in me. As I laid on my back, and she pinched my wrist with her fingers, she said my pulse was stronger, and not as slippery as the first day I showed up at her door.

"But you're still grieving," she added. "That is why some of the needles are sore and tight. They are holding on – when really, you need to let go."

I immediately thought of my Mom. Is that what she was referring to?

She had me turn over, and she massaged my back with her aromatic perfume of oils. But before she left, she lit some earthy Chinese herbs and fanned the smoke throughout the room. Then she quietly closed the door *as I gently opened a window in the cabin.*

Chapter 24

LOTUS

My bare feet felt smooth on the wooden floors, and the light coming through the windows was warm. The sea breeze carried itself into the main room, where I plopped down into the faded armchair. The book in my hand was one I had taken from the bookcase – The Prophet, by Kahlil Gibran. I flipped a few pages to the center and landed upon these lines:

Say not, 'I have found the truth,' but rather, 'I have found a truth.'

Say not, 'I have found the path of the soul.' Say rather, 'I have met the soul walking upon my path.'

For the soul walks upon all paths.

The soul walks not upon a line, neither does it grow like a reed.

The soul unfolds itself, like a lotus of countless petals.

That was it – I was unfolding like a lotus. Grand wisdom doesn't come in a flash of lightening, personal transformation doesn't happen overnight, and healing doesn't take place in a hospital. I could see that now.

Instead, the process of becoming was one in which the layers of life must be pulled back one at a time. With each layer of exposure, new depth and clarity is found; with each petal comes beauty.

The lotus surrounds itself with water, and it protects its center at night. Only when the sun shines down on it fully does it feel safe enough to open. When it does, it sighs a whisper of complete surrender, stretching itself into a reflection of the sun – like God looking in a mirror.

Is this what I was doing? Watching myself from the warmth of the beach, trying to find safety in order to reach wisdom?

I didn't know what was real any more – this cabin or the little room on "D" Street? I could no longer tell what I should focus on – the lump or the things I needed to change in my life? And the little blue pills – were they doing anything at all if I could miss a dose and not realize it?

I didn't have the answers, but I felt I was at least making progress by finding the questions.

I put the book back on the shelf and stepped out onto the deck. Seagulls dove down at the white caps, and their squawk was enough to pierce my ear drums. Sandy slept next to the door, and Jim sat quietly next to her, contemplating the horizon.

*"I'm very proud of you," he said, "for coming here and looking for answers. You're **Adding Honor** to the world around you. You're honoring your path – you're honoring yourself – and in turn, you're honoring your families."*

I was surprised to hear him talk of such things, and my face said as much. I sat down next to Jim on the deck, cross-legged, and I brushed some sand away from the weathered floorboards around me.

"You first have to take care of yourself if you have any desire to be of use to others," he continued. "And the best way to do that is by honoring who you really are, allowing yourself to feel whatever comes up inside of you, and loving yourself enough to know when to let go. When you do those things, you end up bringing honor to those around you – to your families."

"My families?" I asked, tilting my head his direction. "Plural?"

"Yes, your families," Jim restated. "We are part of many families – our immediate family, our friends, our work family, our church family, our clubs and organizations. All of them are types of families that we are a part of. If you think of your life as a tree, you'll notice the many branches that veer off from the base – they are more than just acquaintances, they are kin. God made us all to be brothers and sisters, parents and children – regardless of whether we are blood related or not.

"So, when you do something for yourself, you're really doing it for your family. And when you bring honor to your family, you bring honor to God. You see how it all comes full circle?" he asked, with a glowing smile on his face. I nodded.

"Therefore, bring honor to your family name. Be proud of who you are and where you come from; who you belong to and where you're going. Be proud of those around you, too. Remember, they need just as much encouragement as you do – many times, even more. And lastly, don't forget to encourage yourself as well."

"Sometimes that's hard to do," I said.

"I know," he answered. "But remember the lotus – the one you just read about." My eyes widened with surprise.

"Lotus seeds are rare species," Jim continued. "They can patiently sit and survive for more than two hundred years without any water. When the drought ends and the rains come, they make their way through the mud and the muck, until finally they shoot up towards the sky. I can't imagine their path is an easy one."

"Nor is it rushed," I added, without realizing I had. Jim smiled, knowingly.

"Nor is it rushed," he agreed.

Chapter 25

LIGHT

Everyone in our family had taken different paths after my Mom died. My Dad took to drinking, trying to fill a void that would forever stay empty. My sister flew half way across the continent and busied herself with another degree and research. And I simply stayed in a bad relationship and wasted my time at a dissatisfying job. Who was I to judge any one of us?

My mother's death hit each of us hard. She had been the glue that held us together, and now she was gone. Not only did she die, but she suffered – badly – and there was nothing any of us could do about it. Why is it that a healthy woman with a bright spirit – bright as a shining light – can be taken away by a disease that no one understands? What did she ever do to deserve an ending like that? Before my mother's diagnosis, cancer had just been a word *other* families dealt with. But now it was making its way through mine; first my Mom, and now me. Why, God, why?

Whenever I stop what I'm doing and recall those days, I can still see my Dad sitting next to Mom's recliner, holding her hand while the chemo slowly slid through her veins. He looked hopeless, defeated, and completely lost. But he sat there anyway, never missing a treatment or a doctor's appointment; convinced that all that time spent at the hospital would eventually be cashed in for several more healthy years. He was wrong.

Then there was my sister who believed she might find a cure, devoting all her spare time to research and lab rats. Her post-doctorate degree had originally been in bio-something or other, but after Mom's lump appeared, she quickly switched gears and dove in with everything she had. Clearly, no breakthroughs were made.

My reaction, however, was slightly different. Some might call it naivety or denial, but I honestly didn't think my Mom would die. She might suffer – yes; but leave me – simply not an option. I know it may sound shocking, but I just couldn't go down that road in my own mind. It was probably the only time in my life when I truly lived in the moment and didn't have the courage to plan any further.

Where was Mom in all of this? I truthfully can't remember. I don't know if we even asked her. I think we had been so busy comforting ourselves that we left her on the back burner, staying completely oblivious to what she might have been feeling or wanting. But like the trooper that she was, she simply kept on keeping on.

Every morning when I walked into her room to check on her and pull back the blinds to let the light in, she always did her best to welcome me with a smile – even when she was in pain. She would ask me about my day, even if she couldn't sit up, and she never shooed me away – not once. Even on her worst of days, she fulfilled her role as my Mom. She worried about Dad; making sure my sister and I took care of his needs, as well as our own. And when it looked like she would probably pass before the end of the year, she made me promise to string the holiday lights around the front of the house – and not to forget.

"The holidays are magical," she always told me, from the time I was little. "Nothing can dim their light – not the cold, not worries, not even death. You just have to believe."

And so, I put up the lights and plugged them in – despite my Dad's anger and my sister's protests; they felt I was being insensitive to the seriousness of Mom's situation. But Mom and I knew the truth – whether it was for Santa's benefit or the angels in Heaven, our house was going to shine the way. And one week before Christmas, Mom followed the lights to where they led; Dad tore them down the next day.

None of us were right – Mom didn't live. But none of us were wrong either; we simply grieved and dealt in our own ways. We each honored our own paths, and it was time that I accepted that.

And just like that, with the spring sun beating down on me, another petal gently opened towards the light.

Chapter 26

FALLING

Relationships are such tricky business. Sometimes they jump up and grab you, and before you know it, you're falling head-over-heels in love with someone you barely know. Other times they pull you down, and you're once again falling – but this time it's out of love instead of into it. When that happens, the higher self inside of us knows we should let go and move on, but the scared little ego can't deal with such uncertainty, and so we stay put. We make excuses for bad behavior on the part of the other (or sometimes even ourselves), and we turn a blind eye to the obvious signs right in front of our face.

I'd been dating the same guy for a number of years, and though the first year was sweet and romantic, and ones that followed were a bore and unhealthy. But when my Mom was sick, I decided it was better to have someone around to lean on verses no one at all. Looking back, I don't know if that was the right decision or not.

I remember being extremely irritated about Jake being present the day my Mom passed. The moment was a personal one, and I really didn't want him there. But he was, and there was nothing I could do about it. Months later I found myself becoming angry that he got to partake in such a gift. He didn't deserve it; he didn't even like my mother.

His true colors really started to shine a few days after Mom had died. I was having a hard time dealing with her loss and my family's response to it, and I asked Jake to come be with me. He was too busy, however, getting high with his roommate and heading out to an all-night kegger. What a prince.

He got angry with me when I wasn't in the mood to get physical, and he had little patience for my grieving process. But even then, I still didn't end it. I couldn't. I was too scared to be alone.

And so now here I was, a couple years later, stocked with Costco bottles of pain killers, prescriptions of anxiety pills, and boxes of cheap red wine. Something needed to change.

Chapter 27

QI

"Ahh," the little old lady said with a twinkle in her eye. "You have come to an important cross in the path."

"I have?" I asked, lying on the massage table, face up, watching the sparkle that seemed to be coming from her pupils.

"Oh yes," she continued, "I can feel it in your pulse; your *qi* is flowing more rhythmically now. Not as much blockage as before."

"My what?" I asked, quizzically

"Your *qi*," she repeated. "Like the word *cheese*, but without the *z*." My face still must have shown its confusion. "*Qi* is your life force – the energy flowing through your spirit and your body. Everything and everyone are filled with *qi*. When we are healthy and peaceful, our *qi* flows freely, like a beautiful waterfall. But when we are ill or stressed, our *qi* gets blocked, like a damn."

"What does my *qi* look like?" I asked.

"You're somewhere in between," she replied, lowering my wrist back onto the table and positioning herself on the little stool next to me. "But when you first arrived at my door a few days ago, your *qi* was locked up in a box so tightly, nothing could free it. I'm quite pleased to see you've taken the lid off that box once again."

She inserted a few more needles into my ear and forearms, finishing off with a few around my shins and ankles. She slowly placed her hand on the top of my head and gave me a gentle grin before leaving me to rest and heal.

I closed my eyes and breathed deeply, as I had done several times before, inhaling and exhaling *in rhythm with the waves.*

Chapter 28

DUST

"It's time," Jim said.

"I know," I replied.

We sat there looking out at the horizon for a long time, neither of us saying anything more. Jim didn't need to mention Jake's name; I already knew where he was going with this. And he was right; I had known it for a long time. But before now, I wasn't strong enough to do what needed to be done... or so I thought.

*"That's not it," Jim said, as if he could read my thoughts. "You've always been strong enough – your strength has never left you – and it never will. However, it's time for you to Stand Up. You need to **Stand Up for what is Right**, and that begins with You. Something is wrong, and your body is telling you; it will always get your attention as a last resort if you don't heed the earlier warnings. People can be unwell in so many ways; physically, mentally, emotionally, and spiritually. It's time that you bring all of them into balance once again.*

"You deserve so much more than what you've been settling for. You deserve to be loved and cherished, respected and empowered. If you don't have that with this man, then move on. Cut your losses, shed a few tears, take a deep breath, and start a new chapter. Tell the universe you want more – deserve more – and then prepare yourself for its arrival."

The breeze blew harder, as if in agreement with Jim's words, brushing my hair away from my face like a new clean slate.

146

"Jim," I asked, somewhat cautiously, "have I been wasting my life away with Jake all this time?"

"No, sweetie," he reassured me. "Remember the good times in the beginning, and don't forget the lessons he taught you along the way. It was valuable time, not lost time. There is no point playing the 'what if' game, there is only what we learn from being a participant."

I nodded my head in understanding, still looking out at the waves.

"Also," Jim added, "don't forget to Stand Up for others as well. We're all in this adventure together. Sometimes we have to speak for those who have no voice – we have to speak the Truth, and shelter anyone who feels unsafe. We must empower the ones who are scared, and celebrate those who believe they are alone. In doing this, we bring everyone up to the Great Table to feast – not just a few – and in turn, we all get to enjoy the Gifts of this life.

"Before you know it, and when you least expect it, little treasures with your name on them will start *appearing in your pathway, too. But to make room for them, you need to give your life a good spring cleaning – dust out anything or anyone who is no longer adding to your soul. Air out the stuffy rooms of your heart that have been locked up and forgotten about. Throw open the windows of your spirit and let in all the vibrant light you can stand." He smiled, and then gave me a little wink. "I believe you know where to start."*

Chapter 29

MILESTONE

I didn't wait to reconsider. I went ahead and broke off my relationship with Jake after I got home from acupuncture. He didn't seem all that surprised or upset about it, though he did try to give me a bit of a guilt trip over ruining our weekend dinner plans.

The following morning when I awoke, I reached for the jumbo bottle of pain meds out of habit, as I always did, and all of a sudden it dawned on me – I had no headache; first time that had happened in as long as I could remember.

I smiled.

And just like that I crossed one very important task off my to-do list.

Chapter 30

TEA

The tea kettle whistled, letting me know it was ready to pour boiling water over fragrant jasmine leaves. While I waited for the tea to steep, and as the gentle aroma danced throughout the air, I started thinking about my job – the one that seemed oceans away.

Since breaking up with Jake, a new breath of fresh air had come into my being, and it awakened all my senses and muscles, urging me forward in all sorts of directions.

I cleaned my apartment and threw out old magazines that hadn't been perused in months. I sorted through my closet and made a pile of clothes that I would later donate to the Women's Shelter downtown. I even wrote a happy little poem in my new journal. It was short, nothing too special, but it was sweet.

All these thoughts were with me while I sipped hot tea in the beachfront cabin. The one thought that felt heavier than the rest, however, and that just wouldn't budge, was the office. If I were to take Jim's advice, I would have to stand up for myself not just in my relationships, but also at work. Sadly, though, so many others had already done that with no positive results to show for it. We were dealing with a boss who was nothing less than a bully, using intimidation and fear as motivators instead of praise and support. We were all miserable – working long, stress-filled hours – and we believed we were wasting our lives away in a building that did very little to nurture our souls.

I kept sipping my jasmine green tea, watching seagulls dive at the waves, when there was a knock at the door. I didn't bother getting out of the armchair since I had a decent guess about who it was, and Jim went ahead and let himself in.

"Time to start teaching!" he announced, enthusiastically.

"What are you talking about?" I asked, a bit annoyed that he was disturbing my quiet time.

"Now that you're beginning to really Live the life you were meant to, it's time you help others to do the same. Are you the only one who's unhappy at your office?" he asked.

"You know I'm not," I replied. "We're all pretty miserable."

*"Then it's time for you to set the example. That's the next step on your path to healing – **Teach by Example**. If you want to see changes, you need to be part of the*

change as well. If you want others to act differently, you should model that behavior to them.

"Take your boss for example. Perhaps he's nothing more than a hurting soul. You never know why people act in hurtful ways towards others, but you can pretty much guess that if they do, then they're in need of love. Just imagine what might happen if all of you started treating him with kindness and compassion instead of running from his presence when he comes into work. Maybe he's lonely, or suffering, and the only way he knows how to feel is by lashing out. You could help him get back to a place of being respectful and nurturing. You could show him a different way out. Remember, everything is either Love or fear, and even then, fear can always be transformed by Love."

I believe Jim knew this was a pretty big order he was asking me to fill. He didn't push me, but when he saw my wheels turning – the spark of hope he was watching for – he nudged me with his shoulder.

"What have you got to lose, kid?"

I could tell he was waiting for me to respond.

"Teach him how to brew tea," Jim continued.

"Excuse me?" I asked, completely confused by his comment.

"When you brew tea, it's a process – it takes time. Show him the same is true with self-development; help him along. Maybe he simply doesn't know the first thing about leading a team of professionals. Maybe he doesn't know anything about management at all. So help him.

"Teach him how to first boil the water, making it so hot that unhealthy substances will burn away, leaving a powerful liquid that will excite anything it touches with intense heat. Then show him how to pick the right leaves, or colleagues, ones that will help him towards his goals. Finally, explain to him about patience – the art of waiting – which allows all of you to do what you do best. When the tea is finally brewed – and the project is complete –

remind him that if he adds just a touch of sugar then everyone can celebrate the sweetness of success."

"Ok," I stared in. "But what if I do all that, and he's still a monster to work for? Then what?"

"Then you leave," Jim confirmed, with a playful sigh of surrender. "But Love is always worth a try first," he concluded. "You'd never believe how many problems have been solved with a little Love."

After Jim left, I ran my eye over the titles on the shelves and pulled a small notebook out of the case. Flipping through to the center, I landed on a page that had obviously been waiting for me. The stanzas were handwritten in black ink – not ballpoint, but a fountain pen – making me wonder how long it had been sitting there.

> ***In every man's heart there is a well***
> ***A deep and dark, fear-filled well***
> ***Little Ollie lost his way***
> ***And into the darkness he fell one day***

A doctor of medicine walked by
And heard little Ollie cry
Please help me, my heart is so ill
But the doctor simply threw him some pills

The priest from the local church looked in
And Ollie swimming in his sin
Father, please help me, I'm lost
But he walked off after making the sign of
        the cross

Then little Winnie came through
Her love for little Ollie was true
Two little souls in this world
One's a little boy, one's a girl

Winnie looked down into the well
And heard little Ollie yell
Winnie, please help me, you're my friend
So she climbed up onto the well and jumped in

Winnie, you must be insane
Why did you do such a thing?
Now we are both stuck down here
Surrounded by all of my fear

Ollie, you may be right
But you forget that I bring the light
I have been here before
Take my hand, I will show you the door

In every man's heart there is a well
Like the one in which little Ollie fell
But Light always dries up the doubt
And Love always shows you the way out

I closed the notebook and let it sit in my lap as I looked out the window. The words of love and forgiveness, second chances and grace were all there within those lines. They spoke to me not only of my difficult boss, but also of my own life – the pills, the lack of

158

faith, the darkness and loneliness. And yet all it took was one other little soul to make a difference and change everything; it only took one other to bring the Light.

I let these thoughts and feelings sink in a bit longer, not moving from the comfortable sagging chair I slouched in. Nonchalantly I looked back over at the bookcase, and like a spotlight out of nowhere, the title <u>On Light Alone</u> beamed towards me, reaching out to take my hand. I got up from where I'd been sitting and let the notebook take my place in the chair. Walking up to the book on the second shelf, I took it down, reverently. While running my fingers along the edge of the pages, I felt something sticking out. Flipping open the page, I discovered a pressed leaf; brick red and perfectly intact. It was stuck to a passage that had been highlighted with a yellow marker, and someone had sketched a lopsided star in the margin.

Whatever she was feeling, whatever her own needs, she was doing love. It was after all, for that she believed she was still here.

It was like hearing the voice of Truth and recognizing it immediately. Life is all about "doing love" – that's why we're here; and that's why I'm still here. As long as I still had "love to do," I wasn't going anywhere. Had that been part of my thought process when I decided to stay, as Jim put it? I hadn't really thought of it like that, but I guess it was.

Is that what the title meant? – On Light Alone. Was I to try and live on Light and Love; basking in a weightless glow, void of fear and loneliness, stripped of unhealthy relationships and pathways, filled with hope, laughter, and possibility?

Looking for the answer or some form of confirmation, I flipped back a few pages. There were no more leaves or highlighted passages, but I did land on a quote from <u>365 Tao</u> that grabbed my attention. I'll admit it was the word cat *that first caught my eye, but as I made my way through the meditation, I began to see myself between the lines.*

Look at the cat
as she stretches out contentedly in the sun.
There is no
thought of the next moment,
only the sheer enjoyment of the present.
Rest assured that she will still be able
to clean herself, to catch mice, to do
all the things that a cat must do.
But she is without anxieties

*The passage went on to say that because she sheds herself of any type of stress, she is able to "**purely and totally**" be who she is meant to be.*

She acts as if she were nature's favorite.
And who is to say otherwise.

That's was it! That was who I was meant to be. I knew it now; I could see it clearly. I was mean to "do love"— without anxieties – and to believe I was nature's favorite, deserving all the best in life. Jim was right, Kahlil was right, the writer of this little book was right; they were all leading me down the same path – the one that lead to "sheer enjoyment of the present." I was bubbling over, I was so excited; and then a sobering thought hit me square in the face – was I too late? Had I waited too long to live the life I was meant to?

I could feel the palpitations start up within my heart, and a solid heaviness pushed down on my chest; I couldn't breathe.

"No!" I cried out in the little room. "No, it can't be too late. I'm not done yet."

"Are you finished telling yourself what you need to hear?" I heard from directly behind me.

I spun around, completely shocked; I thought I had been alone. Instead, there stood Jim. Where in the world did he come from?

Chapter 31

TOUCH

I stared at the ceiling, counting the tiles, as the
Asian woman pinched off the needles in my arm. She
didn't say anything, and neither did I; silence was
understood. But instead of leaving me so I could take my
time getting up and dressing, she pulled her stool from the
corner over to the edge of the massage table. Gathering
herself together, she sat down and took in a couple deep
breaths. I tilted my head slightly to the right to see what
she was up to, and watched her eyes as they scanned

across my chest and abdomen. What was she doing, I wondered.

Her hands were folded gently in her lap, and she repositioned herself a few times to get comfortable. Then her eyes strayed until they were looking into mine.

"Breathe with me," she said, quite reverently. And so I did.

She moved her hands up to my chest, placing one over the lump and the other over my heart, and then she closed her eyes. I wasn't the least bit bothered that she was touching me so intimately, and so I quite naturally lowered my eyes as well. Our breathing ebbed and flowed together, and I noticed her hands doing the same; rocking in an ever so slight sway. Warm heat radiated from her palms, and even though my eyes were closed, I felt my heart and breast begin to glow.

We must have stayed positioned like that for quite some time. When I finally opened my eyes again and looked at the woman, I found her hunched over – like

something heavy was weighing down on her shoulders –
and her face scrunched up in concentration. Her eyes
were still closed, but her hands had stopped rocking over
my body; instead they laid flat and still. Then all at once,
the muscles and wrinkles that surrounded her eyes and
forehead released. She tilted her head skyward with her
eyes still closed, raised her eyebrows, and nodded at no
one in particular.

When she brought her head back down, she opened
her eyes.

"See you tomorrow," she said, taking her hands
away from me, and then putting the stool back in the
corner.

"Wait – please wait," I replied. She turned back
towards me, her tongue rolling around in her mouth like
she was trying to move a piece of stuck food. "What just
happened?" I asked.

"We'll have to wait and see," she answered. "See
you tomorrow," and then she closed the door behind her.

Chapter 32

GRACE

Water from the showerhead cascaded over my body as I brought my left hand up to the space right below my arm. Without looking down, I moved my hand, slowly, until it was over my breast. Taking a deep breath, and then swallowing the lump in my throat, I lowered my hand over the area where the mass was forming. I held the air in my lungs for a moment, and then started taking little shallow breaths. At first it was like touching something scary, something hurtful or dirty. But I kept my hand over the side of my breast, and eventually felt my shoulders relax under the warmth of the water. My breathing calmed and my hand became less stiff; cupping my breast instead of laying flatly over it.

As I stood there, quietly holding myself, I thought back to when the old woman touched me earlier. The radiating heat from her hands had been more than simple energy – more than just *qi* – it had been *magical*. And then it hit me – what I had felt pulsating from her palms and fingers was Love; she actually poured her Love *into* me. I don't know how else to describe it or even how to explain it.

An envelope of Grace wrapped itself around me as soon as I came to this realization, and for the first time since the arrival of the lump, I felt complete Peace. It was like a cloud of down feathers insulated every cell in my being, and a soft glowing light shown on the surface of my skin. With my arm across my midsection, I cupped my breast as compassionately as I could, and I tilted my head down towards it; then I rocked, gently.

A somewhat sly smile formed on my face, and my heart raced. Am I crazy, or did something miraculous just happen? All I can say is that in that moment, with hot water cascading over me, I knew I had nothing to worry about, no matter what happened. I knew I shouldn't get too far ahead of myself, but there was simply no denying the new found giddiness that was somehow coming up from deep within my soul. I was too startled with excitement to cry, and so I laughed; first as a chuckle, and then an eruption of volcanic Joy.

I had no need for pain meds or blue pills that night; I didn't even pour a glass of wine.

Chapter 33

NEW BEGINNING

The following morning I had a sudden burst of inspiration. The idea was a little bit extreme, but I decided to just go with it and not over-think it. Instead of staying at my desk during the lunch hour, I grabbed my "chocolate-flavored" Costco brand weight-loss shake and headed out the door. I drove five miles out of town, passing the tiny airport and our one lone lake. Many summer nights were spent around that lake – campfires, keggers, make-out sessions, and even break-ups.

I veered off to the right and pulled my little Honda up to the front entrance of the Humane Society. I was on my way to get a cat.

I had decided that if I was supposed to teach by example, then maybe I needed somebody to teach me first. The poem in my oceanic revere described a cat so invitingly, and a lifestyle that I so desperately wanted for myself, that I figured nothing would suit me better than a furry friend I could call my own. And since I wasn't in the mood to raise a newborn – and healing had become the theme of my life – helping a rescued cat felt like the ideal thing to do.

One couldn't help but to get emotional at the sight of all the abandoned animals in the shelter. Their eyes drew me into them, and I felt guilty when I actually started narrowing down my decision.

But then like the hand of fate or the touch of destiny, the sweetest, fattest, blackest cat I'd ever seen rubbed up against the cage near my feet, getting my attention, and forcing me to bend down to his level. Long white whiskers darted out from his cheeks, and a small patch of off-centered white fur circled around his nose and mouth. His fat little feet were also gloved in white, and his belly – which was far from starving – had a similar shade, making him look like a penguin. I just knew this was my cat; and he knew it, too.

I filled out the paperwork, bought a cat carrier to take him home in, and buckled "Max" in the front seat of my car.

"Maaaaaaaaaaaaaax," I called out to him, saying his name like the sound of the old percolator coffee pot my Mom used to use, while rubbing his nose through the cage window. Max purred and did his best to get closer to my fingers. We were on our way to a new beginning, together.

Chapter 34

CURLS

I could hear giggling; lots and lots of giggling. I walked around the side of the cabin, and to my pleasant surprise, a little 3-year old girl with brown curly hair and big round cheeks bounced up and down on Jim's knees. He held her hands out in front of her so she wouldn't fall off as he whinnied like a horse – which caused a whole new rounds of giggles – and then convened with more galloping. The sunshine coming from their laughter and the joy on both their faces brought a huge smile to mine.

Jim slowed down his horse and took a break from "trotting" to introduce me to his little friend.

"Meet Libby," he said, very proudly.

"Hi Libby," I said, bending down to her level. Her eyes sparkled, and she looked up at Jim for reassurance before jumping down from his lap and wrapping her arms around my lower legs.

My heart melted; Jim smiled.

"That's kids for ya," Jim replied. "They don't ask for much, but they sure do love to give."

Libby unwrapped her arms from my lower body and stood there, staring at me until I sat down. She made her way over to my lap and plopped into the seat I made with my legs. I was mush.

"Children are some of the best reminders of what's important in life," Jim started in as I ran my hands threw Libby's curls. "They remind us to **Be Givers, rather than takers**. They show us that by Giving to others, we actually receive so much more than we could have ever imagined on our own.

"You know, I'm starting to get up there in years," Jim pointed out, "but the minute that little peanut comes into my view, I feel twenty years younger. Her bright little spirit and unconditional love fills me with so much that I feel like I could climb a mountain.

"And when I stop what I'm doing and take a few minutes to give her my full attention – whether that involves rides on an invisible horse or singing songs about farm animals and rowboats – I can see the gift that Libby receives as well, and in turn, it just doubles my own joy. Everything always keeps coming back full circle."

As if on cue, Libby turned around and looked at me. She reached up and touched my face with two of her pudgy fingers. Then she giggled; at what, I have no idea. But whatever it was, it made both Jim and me giggle as well, and just like that, my heart was ready to burst.

There was so much joy and light and love filling up in its chambers that I didn't think I could take any more.

Libby must have read my mind. Her little arms threw themselves around my neck and she rested her big cheek on my shoulder, holding on for dear life. Without hesitation, I held her close to me and rested my head lightly against hers. We were one.

In that instant, I thought back to what Jim had taught me the first time I'd walked the beach with him and Sandy. God really was a part of everything; She even came with big cheeks and curly hair.

Jim beamed as he watched Libby and me embracing, and then he picked up his walking stick, as if getting ready to go.

"One other thing," he added. "Make sure you give to yourself as well. It's totally ok to pamper your own needs and treat yourself from time to time. And one of the best secrets I could ever share with you is the power of saying 'no' when you just don't feel like doing

something. I don't know why it is that everyone acts obligated to say 'yes' all the time. Nine times out of ten, the most loving thing for you to do is to decline an offer or request."

"That's for sure," I agreed, helping Libby stand back on her own two feet. "If there is one thing my anxiety has taught me, it's that I have permission to say 'I can't' and to ask for help."

Jim smiled.

"That a girl, Mary Lou! Now you're learning," and he got himself up onto his own two feet, took Libby's hand in his, and walked into the sunset.

Chapter 35

OFFERING

That night I had the most vivid dream. In it, I was still sick with cancer and about to start chemotherapy treatment. I sat in a blue high-back chair, the kind you find in hospital rooms, and a doctor I had never seen before explained the up-coming procedure to me. She was very pretty, and I thought it wise I discussed this part with a woman; she would understand.

The room was cold, and I kept rubbing my arms to warm them up. I didn't know which questions I should be asking, but the one question I hadn't forgotten was about my hair – *was I going to lose it?*

"There is a good chance you will," the doctor said, smiling as sweetly as she could. "However, there are several options you might want to consider."

"Can I choose the one where it doesn't fall out?" I asked, trying to lighten my uneasiness.

"Sorry, sweetie," she answered, "no can do. But women have found strength in quite a few other creative ways. Some wear beautiful head scarves that they wrap quite elegantly, others prefer sassy hats or baseball caps. Many of my patients try to match their hair to a few wigs and have them all ready before we even begin. It's totally up to you."

None of these sounded very promising to me.

"What if I just leave it and let my hair fall out as it pleases?" I asked. "Maybe it won't be that bad; maybe most of it will stay."

"That's rather doubtful," she carefully answered, touching the edge of my knee. "That's why most women choose to cut their hair short – or even shave it completely – once the treatments begin."

I put my hands up to my face, hiding my eyes behind them. My body felt hot inside. I just couldn't imagine shaving my long hair all the way off.

The doctor gave me a moment to gather myself, and told me she'd be right back. A few minutes later she walked back in the room, but before she did, she waved to a bright eyed little girl in the hallway. The little girl waved back.

"Who's that?" I asked. "She's very cute."

"Isn't she?" the doctor added. "Her name is Jessica. She's five years old, and she has cancer. She's been coming to get treatment for almost a year now."

My heart sank.

"My patients come in all shapes and sizes," she continued, "and cancer doesn't discriminate; it affects us all in one way or another."

"But she looks so normal," I replied. "And she still has all of her hair."

"Oh she's a very normal five year old girl," the doctor said with a smile. "I can assure you of that. But like you, she had to deal with the effects of chemotherapy. Her hair fell out right away when we first started. She, too, is an owner of a wig."

I listened without interrupting.

"The nearby high school had what they called A Hair Drive about a year ago. They invited the local community to drive in their cars for a free wash if they were willing to cut their hair. The locks were then used to make wigs for children who were sick. Pretty cool, huh?"

"I think it's beautiful," I replied, my eyes tearing up.

The doctor smiled.

"I want to do that," I stated firmly. "Can I do that? Can I donate my hair right now? I just know that's the right thing to do. And besides, it will grow back eventually, right?"

"Right," she answered, clearly thrilled that I was moving forward.

My heart felt lighter thinking of little Jessica in her special wig, and all at once I no longer worried about my auburn strands. I was more excited about the good use my hair would go towards in bringing a small piece of normalcy back into a little person's life.

"Bring the scissors, doc," I said with confidence and a smile. "Let's do this thing."

Chapter 36

MOMENTUM

Soft glowing light poured through my windows the next morning, and I awoke feeling renewed and peaceful. I didn't know why, only that I wasn't anxious. Max sprawled out at the foot of the bed, laying his big belly over the tips of my toes. As I rolled over on my pillow, being careful not to disturb Max's sleep, the dream from the previous night came back to me, just on the tip of my consciousness. Squinting my eyes and even closing them at times, I stretched within my mind to remember the

details; first a little girl, then the hospital, and then…
scissors!

In a complete panic, I threw open my eyes. My
hand flew up to the top of my head, dreading what it
would find, expecting to feel nothing but a smooth bald
curvature. To my relief, soft hair draped over my pillow
and brushed my fingertips; I sighed a huge wave of relief.

As I laid there, the rest of the dream came back to
me in full detail. I sat up in bed thinking about its
significance; pulling my knees up to my chin and
wrapping my arms around them, closing my eyes and
replayed the scene in the hospital room. I had been so
sure about cutting my hair off. There was even excitement
in my decision.

That's when I knew I could handle anything that
came next. I knew I had nothing to fear, and on some
unexplainable level, I knew I was going to be all right.

Max stirred, stretching his white paws out in front
of himself, and then climbed his way over the covers to

where I was sitting. His body vibrated and purred as I scratched his head and rubbed his belly, and I couldn't help but smile as I watched him indulge; his joy was contagious.

I opted to skip my breakfast pill, and instead made myself some hot chocolate with marshmallows. I just felt like celebrating.

With a touch of hot melted marshmallow stuck to my upper lip, I opened my journal and started adding to my list of blessings.

– *Max, the puuurfect companion* ☺

 – *My own hair*

 – *People who give their hair to others*

– *Hot cocoa and marshmallows for breakfast*

 – *Feeling at peace*

The day had just begun, and I was already on a roll. It felt good to be alive.

Chapter 37

TRAIL

"Come with me," Jim said as he began to climb the trail with Sandy at his side.

I didn't ask where we were going; I simply knew to follow.

The day had just started, and the morning light over the beach was so bright it was blinding. Though the waves slowly built up speed out in the distance, all the nature around us was still at rest. The birds were quiet, the wind hardly blew, and little streams of light did their best to shine through any crevice or opening they could find.

We walked for a long time, climbing higher and higher on the dirt path; passing huckleberry bushes and moss covered logs, stones of all sizes and a single waterfall. My eyes adjusted to the light as we rose above the tree line and into cooler climate. Eventually, we reached a peak that looked out over the whole bay; the cliff projecting out of the rock like God's hand.

Following Jim's lead, I sat down on the dry ledge next to his walking stick, and Sandy laid her head in my lap.

"We're almost at the end of our journey together," Jim began. "You've traveled a long way, and you've collected several stones to stand on. I know there has been a lot to take in, and some of these steps will take time. So I want you to remember this very important piece

*– just **Do Your Best**. Don't worry about being perfect; no one is. If you were, you'd have no reason to be here."*

My eyes looked at him with skepticism.

"Oh, come on now," Jim responded with a smile. "You know this is just one big classroom, don't you?"

And he gave me a little wink and a nudge.

"As long as you're doing your best, you have no need to concern yourself with what others think or how they might judge. Usually they're just reflecting their own insecurities when they partake in such silliness. Remember, it's the path that matters."

"The path?" I asked.

"You know – the journey, the lesson, personal growth, change – it's the transformation that counts. In the end, it will only be between you and God. It was never between you and them," he concluded.

Grabbing his walking stick and waking up Sandy from her brief nap, Jim gathered himself up from the ground and began to walk back down the path.

"We're leaving already?" I asked. "But we just spent all that time getting here."

"And wasn't the view spectacular?" Jim replied with a beaming smile. "Come on, Mary Lou, you've got Life to get to. You don't want to be late."

I opened my eyes to the little room on "D" Street. Lying on my back, I turned my head towards the wall; I came out of these reveres quicker and quicker each day. Hanging from the nail above me was a Asian watercolor painting, done in mostly black and white, with a touch of green. My head pushed back against the pillow as I realized what I was looking at; it was the cliff I had just been sitting on with Jim.

I sat up to get a closer look, and sure enough, there were even two small figures perched at the edge.

What exactly was going on? What in the world was happening to me?

Chapter 38

COURAGE

I tried being nice to my boss – I really did. Every morning I began the work day optimistically, giving him the benefit of the doubt, and hoping for a pleasant outcome. But it didn't seem to matter how friendly I was or how hard I tried; he was simply a miserable person who was going to make the lives of those around him miserable as well.

Was I doing my best by struggling in a job that was literally killing me? Was I honoring myself by staying? Of course I wasn't.

But up until that point, I hadn't had the courage to imagine something beyond my current circumstances.

"Just do your best, Mary Lou – it doesn't have to be perfect." I could hear Jim in my head, like a personal loud speaker, just for me.

If courage is moving forward even when you're unsure and scared, then I was about to live the definition. I hadn't the first clue as to where I would go or what I would do, but I did feel I could take the first step and make a change. Faith would lead me since I had no roadmap; it would be my compass and my companion.

"Ok, world," I said in grand fashion to the furniture in the room around me. "Where am I meant to go?"

Not more than a moment passed, and then the phone rang; it was my sister

Chapter 39

THE GENERAL

Jim was decked out in a military uniform, complete with spit-shined shoes, a general's hat, and two silver stars on each shoulder. His walking stick had been traded in for medals and pins that hung from his dark blue suit, and on this particular day, Sandy was nowhere to be found. It was just Jim and me.

The sand disappeared, and instead of our usual beach-scape, we stood in the middle of a white light. The *air around us was quiet and calm, and Jim looked a few inches taller than usual now that his back was at attention. I felt a bit underdressed.*

"The time has come for us to say goodbye, Mary Lou," Jim announced most seriously. "You're ready for what lies ahead. You have the tools you need to Live the Life you're meant to enjoy, and you've already made the changes that were once holding you back.

"I pray you won't forget our time together – I know I won't – and I pray you won't forget the steps you've taken to get here."

I stood there, silently, like a soldier defending Truth and Joy.

"Begin each day in gratitude and praise God," Jim began. "Have faith when the days are long, and stay positive in all that you encounter. Honor yourself and those you're connected to, and remember to stand up for what's right. Be a teacher and use your life as an

example, and don't forget to give freely, knowing that's the purest way to receive.

"This sounds like a lot to juggle, but once you begin Living your life from a place of Joy, the Light alone will guide you along the path. First it may feel like a lesson, and then it will turn into a habit, until finally it becomes your way of Being. Don't worry about messing up – just do your best, one day at a time, simply being who you should be."

He paused in his speech, and I took the opportunity to ask the overwhelming question that wouldn't leave my mind.

"Jim," I asked, "what if all of this is just too much for me to handle? Then what?"

*"That's nonsense," he replied without missing a beat. "You listen to be now," he began, looking me square in the eye. "You've got to **Stand Tall, Walk Straight, and Swing Hard – Real Hard**" he said, while*

making a powerful fist with his right hand and displaying his strength. "You hear me?"

I bit my lower lip, inhaled a big breath, and nodded my head in understanding.

"Be like that little mustard seed, Mary Lou, and move mountains. I know you can."

I stood up straight, smiled at Jim, and this time nodded with confidence.

*"**No Excuses, now,** he concluded, **absolutely none.***"

Then he winked at me. A sparkle reflected off his two stars, and then he was gone.

Chapter 40

LAST APPOINTMENT

There were eleven appointments in all. The last one, however, didn't involve any needles.

When I arrived at the house on "D" street that afternoon, the little Asian lady sat on the porch stroking the cat who was sunning himself. He reminded me of Max, who also loved to lay next to the window in the noon-day sun.

"You can sit there," the old lady said, pointing to the floorboards at her feet. I did as she instructed.

Once I was seated on the floor, she handed me a pen and a piece of red paper cut into a square.

"Write down everything you need to let go of," she said. "Everything."

She didn't need to explain anything more to me. I knew what she meant, and I began jotting down my list: the baggage that needed to be dropped from my heart.

I wrote for a long time, sometimes staring off into space until the next piece came to me. The old lady waited, petting the cat and sitting contently in her whicker rocking chair. A few tears appeared on the page as I wrote the names of those who I needed to release, especially my Mom, and I experienced feelings of giddiness when I mentioned my job. After I felt there was nothing more I could add, I handed the paper back to the woman.

"No," she said, "you hold onto it. It's not for me to see."

She got up from her rocker and walked to the edge of the porch. Unused terra cotta pots and recycled cans were stacked neatly in the corner. She picked up a tin can and came back to where I was sitting, and then handed it to me, along with a half-used book of matches.

"Now burn it," she told me, as she went back to massaging the cat and rocking in her chair.

The first match didn't take; I suspected the book was old, or perhaps water damaged. But the second match ignited quickly, and I lit the paper. In a matter of seconds, the words of pain, struggle, and fear I had written were engulfed in flames, and I dropped the burning square into the can. Black smoke, as thick as night, mushroomed up through the top of the can, floating out into the afternoon sun. And then everything calmed – the flames, the smoke, and my heart.

We sat there for some time until the can cooled enough to touch; the old lady kept checking it with her finger. When she was satisfied it could be lifted, she got up and walked down the steps, heading toward the side of the house.

"Bring the can over this way," she said, walking towards the lavender blushes that were now in full bloom; the cat lovingly following beside her. "You can pour those ashes right here," she said, pointing to a section of dirt under the lavender leaves.

"The ash will act as fertilizer for the plants," she explained, "helping them to grow and bloom through every season. Life can take something dark and ugly and turn it into something useful and beautiful. The same is true with you.

"You turned your list of burdens into nothing more than mere smoke – they simply vanished because fear is not real and it cannot hurt you. The tiny bit of soot that remained in the can will be left here. You must leave it behind if you want to move forward. I believe you understand that now," she stated.

"I do," I replied.

"Then we are done," she said, and she headed back towards the house.

There was no goodbye, no last words of encouragement, or a hug for good luck. She simply walked back up the drooping stairs and opened the front door, while the cat went back to sunning itself in the rays of the afternoon.

Chapter 41

GOOD FRIDAY

I've never quite understood why the day of Jesus' crucifixion is called "Good Friday." Some churches refer to it as "Holy Friday," others as "Black Friday," but any way you look at it, it is a day of pain and suffering. Therefore, it didn't at all surprise me when my second biopsy was scheduled for the Friday before Easter.

I was pleased to see the not-so-friendly-who-then-turned-friendly nurse was back to her usual grumpiness.

For some reason that was comforting. The specialist and his headlamp were in rare form, however – almost giddy.

"Did you enjoy your time on "D" Street?" he asked me.

"It was interesting, to say the least," I replied. He smiled. "But yeah, I'm glad you sent me there. If nothing else, I think I'm ready for what lies ahead."

"Great," he responded. "Let's get this party started."

Interesting choice of words, I thought to myself.

The lab tech that had assisted during my first biopsy a couple weeks prior was once again late for the day's appointment. When he did arrive, I tilted my head in surprised, like a knee-jerk reaction. If I didn't know better, I would have thought he was the gardener from the house on "D" Street. I knew I must have been imagining things.

My body buzzed all over as I sat in the reclining chair. Since I already knew what was coming, I wasn't as anxious as before, and I didn't even bother taking my meds that morning either. Whether that had been a smart idea or not, I felt fine when I woke up, and I decided to just go with it.

The repetitive piercing and stabbing of the needle into my breast didn't feel any less invasive than it had the weeks before, and I knew there would be some swelling in the days to come.

As soon as the doctor retrieved his sample, he handed it to the lab tech, who placed it under a microscope. I remained quite peaceful as I waited this time. (I think wearing my favorite bra helped – dusty lavender and lace by Calvin Klein. My sister and I had matching ones.) To help pass the time, I looked around the room; my ice pack sat at the ready on the counter nearby, and a fish mobile had been strung up overhead. I assumed that was to help distract any children who might find themselves visiting this chair.

"Doctor," the lab tech called out, "you might want to have a look at this."

The two of them went back and forth checking the slide, talking in an abbreviated language I couldn't understand. The only thing I could make out was towards the end.

"You're sure?" the doctor asked, more as a request for confirmation than as a question.

"Positive," the lab tech responded, very light-heartedly.

"'Cause I can take another sample," the doctor continued.

"No," said the technician, "that's not necessary. This sample is quite adequate." And then he packed up his little black box and left the room to take my tissue samples to the main laboratory.

Nurse Sunshine, who had been standing next to me the whole time, handed me the bag of ice and helped me position it over my heart and breast. While we were waiting for the specialist to get back to me, I decided to try something.

"You're a really important person in this office, you know," I said looking up at her.

"Excuse me?" she replied, clearly stunned by my comment.

"I said you're a really integral part of this office. So many women must come through these doors every day, right?" I asked. The nurse nodded.

"And all they see," I continued, "are sterile counters, sharp needles, scary headlamps, and very focused men. It's comforting to have a woman in here holding your hand and making you feel safe when you're scared to death of what all these instruments and test results are going to tell you. So, thank you," I said with a smile.

She was so taken aback that she didn't know what to say. She bit the inside of her lower lip, and then I saw her eyes fill up with tears.

"I didn't think anyone noticed," she replied.

"Oh trust me," I insisted, "we notice," and I squeezed her hand as tightly as I could. The nurse squeezed me back and gave me a sincere, heart-felt smile. I had a feeling it was the first of many to come.

Chapter 42

HOPE

On Saturday, I waited. There were no more acupuncture appointments to be had, no more biopsies to be taken; no boyfriends that needed to be called, no work that needed to be tended to, nothing.

I recalled the cover of a book I'd seen in my beach-front reverie; one that had jumped out at me with its bright yellow cover, but which I hadn't actually opened. I hopped in my car and headed downtown, thinking the local bookstore might be worth a try. Bunny decorations and multicolored hanging baskets lined every sidewalk and shop window, and the neighborhood Egg Hunt was in full swing as I drove by.

Surprisingly, the lady at the help desk knew exactly what book I was referring to when I described it. Apparently I hadn't been making things up in my dream. She led me around the corner to the Gift section and pulled a thin soft-back volume off the top shelf.

Hope for the Flowers, she said to me, reading out the title. "Such a sweet little story. Enjoy!" And then she was gone.

I carried the book with me throughout the store until I arrived in the children's section. Plopping myself down in one of the beanbag chairs that were technically for kids to lounge in, I turned the first page and began reading.

About half way through the story of two little caterpillars who are "looking for more," another cute little person with big blue eyes flopped into the chair next to me. In her hands were *The Velveteen Rabbit* and *The Secret Garden*.

How fitting, I thought.

We each smiled and then left the other to their stories.

Her whole insides leapt. 'Butterfly – that word,' she thought. 'Tell me, sir, what is a butterfly?'

'It's what you are meant to become. It flies with beautiful wings and joins the earth to heaven. It drinks only nectar from the flowers and carries the seeds of love form one flower to another. Without butterflies, the world would soon have few flowers.'

'How does one become a butterfly?'

'You must want to fly so much that you are willing to give up being a caterpillar.'

'You mean to <u>die</u>?'

'Yes and no. What <u>looks</u> like you die, but what's <u>really</u> you will still live. Life is changed, not taken away. Isn't that different from those who die without ever becoming butterflies?'

'And if I decide to become a butterfly, what do I do?'

'Watch me. I'm making a cocoon. It's an in between house where the change takes place. It's a big step since you can never return to caterpillar life. During the change, it will seem to you or anyone who might peek that nothing is happening – but the butterfly is already becoming. It just takes time!

'And there's something else. Once you are a butterfly, you can really love – the kind of love that makes new life. It's better than all the hugging caterpillars can do… we're all waiting for you.'

And she decided to risk for a butterfly.

The little girl had left my side by the time I reached the end of the book. The transformational journey of these two little creatures – learning to let go of the familiar, trusting the still small voice inside, and ultimately becoming new creations – seemed so personal to me that I didn't know whether I wanted to laugh or cry.

So, I just went ahead and did both, right there in the yellow beanbag chair.

Chapter 43

GIFTS

Pink marshmallow Peeps and Cadbury mini-eggs made perfect breakfast companions as the sun rose over the city on Sunday morning. Several years back I had come to the conclusion that chocolate mini-eggs were much more my thing than the overly sweet cream-filled ones.

The Easter Bunny surprised Max with a can of tuna in spring water, which I made sure to point out to him, and he thanked me by licking the bowl clean as his belly dragged on the carpet. Heaven forbid he should ever go without food.

Downtown's weekend farmers' market bloomed in full color, even though it was a holiday, so I headed over and indulged in some freshly cut freesia and lilies. White stargazer lilies had always been Mom's favorite; I picked out the prettiest, most fragrant ones.

Several families had already beaten me to the main gates of the cemetery, where tombstone after tombstone was decorated in tulips and daffodils; some even had their own plastic eggs. Little girls in filly dresses and little boys in spring pastels ran through the grass, having not a care in the world whether they were trampling over someone's grave or not. I liked their enthusiasm.

I made my way over to the tall birch tree and sat down on the bench underneath. My sister and I had purchased it after Mom had died, thinking Dad might like to sit there when he came to visit. However, I don't think it had gotten much use.

With water-sprayed lilies in hand, I eventually got myself up and carefully ventured the short distance to Mom's grave. The grounds crew had cut the grass, but someone forgot to collect the clippings. I wiped them away from the stone and ran my hand over Mom's name. "Beloved wife and mother" was written at the bottom. I laid the flowers over her name and then stood back, wiping away a few tears from each of my eyes.

"There's something I need to tell you, Mom..." I started in, and then I began my little story. I whole-heartedly believed she had been with me through every step of the last few weeks, but for some reason I needed to say it out loud. Doing so made it so much more real – both the physical realities and the personal transformation.

When my sister had called a few nights before – claiming she could just "feel" something wasn't right with me – I finally broke down and told her the truth. I had been keeping all of this to myself the whole time, and I realized it was ok for me to lean on others a bit. That was part of honoring myself.

She immediately wanted to catch the next flight out to be with me, but I insisted she wait. I told her I would give her a call the moment I knew anything for certain. In an attempt to show her I was keeping it together, I told her about wearing my lavender bra to the last biopsy. She loved it.

However, I still didn't say anything to my Dad. In all honesty, I wasn't sure he could handle it.

I showed up at his door after visiting Mom, and was beyond pleased to find him looking perky and painting the house!

"Wow, Dad – what's gotten into you?" I asked, completely stunned.

"You know, sweetie, I just thought this place could use a lick of paint," he answered back, coming down the step ladder and wiping his hands on his t-shirt before coming over to give me a great big bear hug. "Aren't you a sight for sore eyes," he added, planting a little peck on my check.

I carried the lilies and freesia into the kitchen and filled up one of Mom's old crystal vases with water, placing the display on the counter.

"Mom's favorites," I said as I arranged the blossoms.

"Yes, I know," answered Dad, "I remember well." And for the first time in as long as I could remember, he wasn't crying as we talked about Mom. "Speaking of which, Peanut," he continued. "I have something for you."

He disappeared into the back room, and when he came back to the kitchen, he was holding a small lapel pin in his hand.

"I found this the other day when I was going through some old things in the bedroom. It was your Mother's, and I thought you might like to have it."

He placed the little pin in the palm of my hand ever so gently, waiting for me to say something, but I was too stunned to respond.

It was a pink lotus.

Chapter 44

RESURRECTION

I pulled into the corner mini-mart on my way home from visiting my Dad. Max was almost out of cat food and I'd been meaning to pick some up; the fluffy guy ate like he wasn't going to see food again for a few days. With Mom's beautiful lotus pin fastened to my sweater, I walked lightly into the store, and almost knocked over the corner display. As I tried to balance myself, my arm swung right into a customer heading for the checkout counter.

"Oh! I'm so sorry," I cried out before I could even get my bearings.

"Mary Lou?" the man answered back

"Oh my gosh – Hi!," I replied; it was the doctor – the specialist. "I didn't recognize you without your… your um… I mean…" I stumbled over my words.

"It's quite all right," he said, calming my frazzled speech. "In fact, I was going to call you."

"You were?" I asked, quite surprised.

"Yes," he said, with a huge beaming smile coming from his face. "I have wonderful news – amazing news, actually."

I held my breath, bracing for whatever was about to come next.

"Well," he started in, "I'm not really sure how to explain this…"

"Yes...?" I asked; my heart beating faster. "Please, whatever it is – just tell me."

The cancer was gone.

Epilogue

There was no scientific explanation for what had happened. One day there were cancer cells in my body; and the next day there weren't. The specialist, though beyond thrilled with the news, couldn't figure out what had happened. And yet, he must have known something like this was possible, or else why would he have sent me to the house on "D" Street in the first place?

A wave of overwhelming relief and joy poured over me when he said the words, causing me to hug the doctor in an almost crushing embrace. However, I must admit, his news wasn't entirely surprising. So much had taken place in the days between February 29th and March 27th that I started to believe nothing was impossible anymore.

February 29th – Leap Day – truly was a day of Grace. It was that extra little day that showed up only one time every four years, and this year it had a gift for me. Some might not think of a cancer scare as a Gift, but I had learned otherwise.

I called my sister the moment I got home, asking Max to be patient with me just a little longer; his food would be coming soon. We cried together on the phone, and made plans for her to come out the following week.

Even though I had no need for chemotherapy or radiation, the doctor wanted to remove the lump regardless. I was more than happy to oblige, but when I reached my hand up to my breast and felt it one more time, I became sad. In a very unique way, it had become like my little friend – leading me down the path to New Life.

Towards the end of our phone conversation, my sister and I came up with a second plan: I would move across country to live with her. There was nothing holding me back, and the change of lifestyle and scenery would do me good. She even had a single friend she was dying to introduce me to. I laughed and told her I might hold off a bit before jumping back into the dating ring. For the time being, Max and I were turning out to be excellent partners.

We told each other "I love you," and hung up the phone. She headed back to her lab in search of a cure for cancer, and I was still in desperate need of getting food for Max. I knew I would pass "D" street on the way to and from the market, so I decided to pick up one more bouquet of lilies. I wanted to say thank you to the little Asian woman who helped me change my life.

However, no one answered the door when I knocked, and the cat that usually sat near the porch was nowhere to be found. The whole scene felt odd.

I placed the flowers just inside the screen door and headed back down the lop-sided steps one last time. The gardener who'd I'd seen every day for the last week and a half was working intently on his perennials. I was about to ask him if he'd seen the old woman when something stopped me in my tracks.

Lying at my feet sat the most perfectly smooth oval rock, speckled black and white, just like the one in my reverie. I picked it up and held it in my hand. Like before, the solid rock warmed inside my touch, vibrating heat through my palm and fingers. Memories of the beach came flooding back until I realized the gardener was standing in front of me.

"Mary Lou," I heard the familiar voice say, causing me to look up in complete surprise.

A yellow-winged butterfly flew up between us, and fluttered around the fragrant hedge of lavender.

My hand dropped, along with the object in it, and I stared at him in amazement and awe, as the heavy stone gently rolled away.

A Note from the Author

I have always been my Father's daughter.

In June of 1995, my Dad – James Elias Simon – passed away at the age of 61 from cancer. In his short but full life, my Father used his charismatic passion and deeply felt respect for others to inspire multitudes of people, while empowering those who normally stood at the sidelines. He earned the titles of Doctor, Major General, and Undefeated Arm-Wrestling Champion, but everyone simply called him "Jim" – from the kids in the neighborhood to the little old ladies at church. He honored the lives and culture of his Lebanese immigrant parents; faithfully and gently loved his wife and children; and left behind a legacy of kindness, humility, and God-loving strength.

Dad also passed along his personal Code of Conduct – one he used every day for most of his adult life. This simple yet profound Code has touched the lives of many throughout the world, and continues to live on today.

We love you and we miss you, Dad. This story is for you ~

19 November 1992

My Daily Code of Conduct:

1. Praise the Lord.

2. Put my faith in God, and keep it there.

3. Defend human principles and values.

4. Add honor to our family name.

5. Do my very best always.

6. Teach by example

7. Positive mental attitude always.

8. Be a giver, rather than a taker.

9. Stand tall, walk straight, and swing hard.

10. No excuses, absolutely none.

James E. Simon
Major General, USAFR

Maria Simon is the author of the international hit *I'll Always Walk Your Fish with You*. She has spent the last 20 years teaching, counseling, and empowering young adults through universities, leadership programs and spiritual retreats, while volunteering countless hours for Rotary International, Chrysalis International, and as an international ambassador. She currently teaches at

Mahidol University International College and resides in both the Pacific Northwest and Southeast Asia.

www.maria-simon.net

facebook.com/mariasimon-author